THE McGUFFIN

John Bowen

BALLANTINE BOOKS • NEW YORK

Library of Congress Catalog Card Number: 84-45817

ISBN 0-345-32848-5

This edition published by arrangement with Atlantic Monthly Press

Manufactured in the United States of America

First Ballantine Books Edition: May 1986

*For
Rosemary, Anthony
and Christopher Hanson*

FOREWORD

NONE OF THE CHARACTERS OF THIS BOOK IS INTENDED TO portray any 'real' person, living or dead except insofar as I have used, as any novelist does, bits of my own life to flesh out my narrator. I did, for instance, play Tegeus to Shirley Williams' Dynamene in an undergraduate production of *A Phoenix Too Frequent*, and I did, as a child, have a cat which died in the manner described on page 129.

There is no Statler Hotel in Vaduz, and, although the cinema is much as I have described it, I have no reason to believe that its owners would ever allow it to be used for a Pornographic Film Festival, nor do the films shown and people involved in my imagined Festival at all resemble those of the Locarno Film Festival, which I attended in 1983. I first invented the *Radical* for my novel, *Storyboard*, which was published in 1960, and has been long out of print. The B.B.C. Television programme described in this book clearly has some similarities with an actual B.B.C. programme (it would be difficult to devise a credible programme which did not), but T.V. programmes, I suggest, are fair targets for parody, and I have never, as far as I know, met any of the admirable people concerned with its production, and no character of this book is intended to represent, or may be construed as representing, any of them.

My thanks are due, and gratefully given, to the following people, many of them friends, for information, advice and assistance:

Philip French of the B.B.C. and the *Observer*, Derek Hill

and Paul Madden of Channel Four, and David Streiff, Artistic Director of the Locarno Film Festival, for films and Festivals.

John Lumbers of Banbury Upper School for photography and John Jennings of Saint Martin's College, Lancaster, for an experiment in making black-and-white enlargements from colour negatives by means of a slide-projector in the manner I have described.

Dr Patrick Woodcock for medical matters.

Richard Brain of the *Times Literary Supplement*, who arranged for me to watch the paper being printed, and all those of his colleagues and the printers who assisted him in explaining what was going on.

David Cook, who has heard every chapter read aloud, and has made a number of helpful suggestions.

I have found John Russell Taylor's biography of Alfred Hitchcock, *Hitch* (Abacus Books) extremely useful, and have also relied on Leslie Halliwell's *Filmgoers' Companion* (Granada).

John Bowen

REAR WINDOW

I BECAME CONVINCED THAT THE SECOND WOMAN WAS NOT A woman at all.

I live on the top floor of a house in South Kensington. Two houses of a terrace have been combined, and turned into flats. My flat was once the attics of both houses, where the servants slept in the days when such houses kept such servants. I write 'my flat' because I live there alone; my wife no longer lives there. I write my wife, but she was not, at this time, my wife or anybody's wife: she chose not to live in a dependent or even companionable way with any male person. I miss her company, and was not conscious of her being dependent while we lived together. It seems to me that I was the more dependent, and would still prefer to be. Self-pity! Start again.

Behind the terrace are gardens, not the communally owned Gardens which abound in Kensington and Chelsea, but individual back-gardens appurtenant to the tenants of the ground-floor and first-floor flats, and beyond them, separated by a brick wall on which clematis has been trained, are back-gardens to the houses of another terrace. There are trees in many of these gardens, horse-chestnuts imprudently planted when the gardents were young, and now grown over-large, as trees do in towngardens. In spring the candelabra of the horse-chestnuts are white or deep-red, and all through summer the leaves are thick, turning to brown and gold in the autumn when the branches are loaded with the spikey cobs of conkers, but in the winter, when those branches are bare and the grimy wall is no longer

1

concealed by clematis, I can see from my kitchen window into the rooms of the houses opposite; this is especially easy on a grey winter's day when those rooms are lighted. At night, of course, the curtains are usually drawn, and one cannot see into those rooms at all.

I write 'kitchen window' because one does not stand at the bathroom or bedroom windows, looking out; that might be noticed by those living opposite, and thought strange. But the kitchen sink is below the kitchen window in my flat, and it is natural to stand there while washing dishes, trying to keep one's back straight in accordance with the Alexander Method of posture-control, and not hunched over the bowl. I usually wash up after breakfast. A 24-hour accumulation of dishes is cost-effective in terms of the use of detergent and hot water.

I shall describe exactly what I saw. There were two women and an alsatian dog in a lighted room on the first floor of the house opposite. I knew one of the women. She was old, a pensioner in expensive furs. I had seen her sometimes in the street, walking with the help of two metal sticks, attached to her arms. She surprised me once by saying suddenly as I passed her, 'I don't know how much longer I can keep this up. It's bloody awful being old.' Since then, whenever we met, I would smile at her sympathetically, and sometimes she returned my warm smile coldly, in the manner of a society hostess greeted in the street by an over-familiar tradesman, and sometimes she shook her head angrily, and walked on, stick after stick on the hostile pavement. Also I had glimpsed her through leaves on summer afternoons when she sat in the armchair by her window, and looked down into the back-gardens.

She was sitting in that armchair on this occasion. It was turned to one side, away from the window, half-facing into the lighted room. There was a small table, perhaps a card-table, in front of her: one could imagine her playing Patience. There were no playing cards on the table, however, only a few papers, and across from her the second woman sat, with the alsatian dog at her side. Although I

2

could not see the old woman's face, I knew her to be terrified, both of the other woman and the dog. And I came to believe that the other woman, whose face I could see clearly, was not a woman but a man.

Why did I become convinced of this? In transvestites one notices first an artificiality of the voice, but even if the window had not been closed, they were too far away, down a floor and across two back-gardens, for me to have heard what was being said. (Were they actually speaking at all or sitting in silence? I cannot now remember.) Nothing to do with the hair: even if she were wearing a wig, women do wear wigs. Nothing to do with make-up unskilfully or over-generously applied: again, I was too far away to distinguish such details, had no binoculars, was not even wearing my glasses, which are not needed during washing-up. Nothing (that I can remember) to do with posture: she did not cross her legs like Charlie's Aunt from Brazil, where the nuts come from. Because of my work, I have seen both Ray Bolger and Jack Benny as Charlie's Aunt, and she resembled neither, nor any of Andy Warhol's creations, not Candy Darling, not Jackie Curtis.

She was smoking a cigarette. Perhaps when she put it to and took it from her lips, she held it as a man is said to do, with the fingers over the top, whereas a woman is said to hold the fingers beneath. Or perhaps I have imagined this detail in order to provide evidence for a conclusion already formed. I myself do not smoke, so I am not up in such matters.

Two women and an alsatian dog, sitting together one grey winter's morning in a lighted room. (Well, the dog was not sitting, or not on its haunches like the fox-terrier on the old H.M.V. record-labels, but was couched nobly by the chair of its mistress, the younger woman.) There was no direct evidence that the older woman was terrified, none that the younger woman was a man. Yet I looked across from my own kitchen window, still holding in damp hands the washing-up brush of pink plastic with bristles of battered nylon, and knew that this was so. I do not know how long I watched them. These frames are frozen; time does not pass for those within. Then the young woman looked up and across and, as it seemed, directly at me. Movement returned. I gave my attention hurriedly to the dishes in the bowl, hunching my shoulders in defiance of the Alexander Method so as to assume a less remarkable appearance. When I looked up again, the curtains were drawn.

It was a Thursday morning. I was in no hurry. There was time to finish the dishes, drink a second cup of coffee, have a bath, and think. On a Monday, with Press Showings at ten thirty and two thirty, perhaps another at four thirty, on a Tuesday, with all that and my own copy to write afterwards, or even on a Wednesday, with just a morning showing, I should have had less time to brood.

I think now that I should have brooded nonetheless.

Perhaps someone with another job would not have been as strongly affected, would not have noticed anything odd at all, would certainly not have become obsessed by it. But I am a film-reviewer, which is to say that I am already obsessive. To be required to watch at least five films a week, not films of one's own choice, but what is on release—*Party, Party, Young Doctors In Love, Rocky IV, An American Werewolf in Vienna, Galactic Super-Buddies* and *The Yamaha Kid* all within the space of three days—if one were not obsessed by film, one would go mad. Blind pit-ponies, little children yoked to Victorian machinery, their suffering would be as nothing to that of the weekly reviewer of films if one were not a *collector*, did not, the requirements of the job apart, require *oneself* to have seen everything. In the days when I took holidays, I would (except that my wife restrained me) have visited the cinema daily and paid for entry. I have seen *Tom Jones* with Greek sub-titles which filled the bottom third of the screen and *Carry On Up the Khyber* dubbed into Spanish.

Moreover the act of observing some happening, which may be sinister, through a window with the observer unobserved is itself a *cliché* of film. In *The Window*, on a hot night in New York City, a small boy (Bobby Driscoll) is

4

sleeping out on the fire-escape of the tenement in which he lives, and sees a man being murdered by a neighbour. The body disappears, and the boy, known to be over-imaginative, is not believed. In *Three Ten From Paddington*, Margaret Rutherford as Miss Marple watches from the window of her own railway carriage a murder being committed in a train passing in the other direction. In *Still of the Night*, Meryl Streep is watched performing strange acts with a sinister Japanese. (He turns out to be a masseur; it is all innocent.) There is a silent movie, the title of which vexingly will not come to me, in which the characters are shown as if under continuous photographic observation by the F.B.I. In Brian de Palma's *Hi, Mom!*, the hero's hobby is to photograph people through windows. This last film was made as a piece of direct homage to the classic of the *genre*, which is, of course, Alfred Hitchcock's *Rear Window*.

The hero of *Rear Window* (James Stewart) is a photographer for an illustrated news-magazine, immobilised within his own apartment by an injury to his leg. He is bored. He watches the man who lives on the ground floor of a building opposite having a row with his bedridden wife, and takes a picture. Later the wife disappears, which is to say that he, watching obsessively from the rear window of his apartment, no longer sees her in the rooms on which he is keeping watch. Later still, he sees the man digging in the garden. By this time he and his girl (Grace Kelly) actually want there to have been a murder. They have become murderers by proxy; they want the wife to be dead. This is one of the features which makes the film a classic. Hitchcock is saying that those who watch such films (you and I) are also people of such a sort; we will kill vicariously; we take pleasure in the murder of our fellows. Nevertheless, with or without this interesting sidelight on the darker side of the human *psyche*, the important difference between *Rear Window* and *Still of the Night* is that in *Rear Window* the man *has* murdered his wife.

I shall repeat that. The man has murdered his wife. To begin with, there was only a marital tiff, then an absence of

5

the woman. None of this was proof; even the digging in the garden was not proof. Yet, at the end . . . And all that I myself had seen was two women in a lighted room with an alsatian dog, and I had received certain impressions, which I might myself have induced.

However, I was not immobilised. Lying in the bath, knees raised, head resting against the wall, I examined my legs. They were nothing to write home about, but they were in working order. They could be used to confirm or to disprove my suspicions. What would James Stewart have done, and at what point, if he had had the use of his? One does not ask these questions while watching the film.

I could think of no excuse to go round and knock on the door. Perhaps, next time I passed the old lady in the street, I might murmur, 'Are you alright?' Steam rose from the cloudy bathwater. I imagined that meeting. I would murmur the question conspiratorially, and in consequence not be clearly heard. 'What? What?' She supports herself on the two metal sticks, her head turned towards me, her eyes darting from side to side in fear at being thus accosted by a stranger. 'Are you ALRIGHT?' The queue at the bus-stop has become an audience. Passers-by, even on the other side of the street, cease their progress to the shops, and turn to look. She stumps away, *thump! thump!*, one stick after the other, faster than she should, slower than she wishes, and in her anxiety to leave me behind, falls over, breaking several bones. As I hurry to her assistance, she gives a thin scream. Already the lady at Number Six is telephoning the police.

I left the bath, dried, and dressed. I went to the bedroom, stood at the window, and looked across and down. The curtain was still drawn. I spent much of that day at the bedroom window, watching. The kitchen window would have given a better view of the inside of that room, but as long as the curtain was drawn, this was of no consequence. The closed curtain fuelled my obsession, partly because it seemed to confirm that illicit acts were being performed behind it, partly because its being closed was so unfair; nobody had drawn a curtain on James Stewart. When

6

darkness fell, I could see that there was still light in the room. I spent most of the evening, as I usually do, watching television (there was a showing of *The Lace-Maker* on Channel Four), but broke off during the commercials to check the condition of the window. The light was switched off at some time between eleven thirty and midnight. In the morning, the curtain was still drawn.

You may have concluded that I only work for half the days of the week. That is not so. My work as film-reviewer of the *Radical* does only occupy me for half the week, but no reviewer can live by a weekly column alone; even the reviewers of *The Sunday Times* and the *Observer* have other jobs. The *Radical* is a journal of opinion and analysis, like the *New Statesman* and the *Spectator*, but with a rather smaller circulation; it is directed, as they are, at opinion-leaders, but reaches fewer of them. I am paid fifty pounds a week for my column, with another thirty pounds whenever I am asked to review books on film for the Literary Pages, which may be four times a year. As a weekly wage, it is considerably below the national average, and I supplement it as I can. I provide questions for quizzes on radio and T.V., and broadcast in person, sometimes as anchor-man, sometimes as panel-member, for the World Service of the B.B.C. (It is a skilled craft. One has to speak very slowly, since listeners in South East Asia only hear every third word.) I lecture, at fifty pounds plus reasonable expenses, to Film Societies in the southern counties, and my name is not un-known within the para-academic world of the Polytechnics: I give a twice-yearly course on *Aspects of Film* to extra-mural students at the East Hounslow College of Further Education. (I was asked to extend this to Brentford, but one doesn't get paid unless fifteen students register for the course, and only seven did.) I write books—twenty-seven biographies so far of filmstars for Popular Publications, and was at this time at work on the twenty-eighth (Clint Eastwood), which was a little overdue. One is not paid royalties on the sale of such books, but sells one's copyright for a lump sum, half on delivery, half on publication.

However, these sums can be used to wipe out debt, and the only book for which I have managed to negotiate royalties, my study of Pasolini, *Self-Mutilating Angel*, was remaindered before it managed to earn any. At the time of our divorce, my wife offered to make mc an allowance, but I refused it, and I do not need it now.

Next morning the curtain was still drawn. I could not spend all day watching. I usually go to the *Radical* office on Friday, to pick up my free copy of the magazine and see whether the Literary Editor (who is also the Editor) has any special work for me. There was work to be done on Clint Eastwood. I set myself a weekly target of four A4 pages of triple-spaced typescript (about 1200 words), to be completed on Thursdays and Fridays, so, with Thursday already wasted, I had fallen behind. Also I had some preparatory notes to make for my weekly class at Hounslow, which would itself lead to extra work, since that night's topic was *The Script*, and I was bound to end up with a pile of manuscript, much of it hand-written, to read and assess. I would have dismissed the memory of that lighted room from my mind if I could, but I could not. I stared across from my kitchen window to the closed curtain, and longed for it to be drawn back, for the old woman to take her place at her own window, idly gazing into the back-gardens, best of all for her to look up at me, and wave, to throw open her window, as I would mine, and shout across, 'Isn't it a wonderful day? I really quite enjoy being old and crippled.'

Nothing of that sort happened. The curtain remained closed, and rain dripped from the trees onto soggy lawns. I did not even know the number of the house in which the old woman lived, but I could see the end of the terrace from my window, and if I were to count the houses, and then, on my way to the office, go round to the front . . . It was all madness: excessive solitude was rendering me eccentric. I counted the backs of the houses. The old lady's house was six along from the end of the terrace. Having identified it, I could take a look at the front, and see whether those windows were curtained also. I did not know the name of the old lady, but could discover it, once I had the address, by consulting the Electoral Register in the Chelsea Public Library. If I saw nothing to reassure me when I examined the house from the front, I could knock on the door, make some excuse, and ask for the old lady by name. Behind me the kitchen radio reported strife in Lebanon, sectarian murders in Northern Ireland, a parcel-bomb which had singed the eyebrows of the housekeeper of a learned judge, oil prices in disarray, a run on the pound, allegations of corruption against some special aide of the President of the United States, a collapse of England's cricketers in Australia, nothing out of the ordinary. I was not James Stewart, nor was meant to be.

The Chelsea Public Library is not far from where I live; it is in the King's Road where the old Chelsea Town Hall used to be. The numbering of the houses on my own side of the road is odd; hers, facing the other way, would be even. I did not know from which end the numbering of her terrace began, but the house, six along from the end, must be either Number 12 or Number 36. Several Campbells, probably of more than one generation, inhabited Number 36. Number 12 was divided into two maisonettes, of which one contained only one elector, Forbes-Duthie, Meralda L.

Leaving the Public Library, I was already later than usual for my visit to the office. Of course, I do not have to go to the office at all on Fridays. There very seldom are letters or odd jobs, and my free copy could be posted to me. I go because I like to make an appearance, to remind them that I am on the staff; it would be so easy to forget, and to appoint someone else as film-reviewer. There is no job-security, no redundancy-pay, no Golden Handshake. Although I have been eighteen years in the job, they could find someone else tomorrow, and the whole basis of all my other jobs as 'distinguished film-critic' would fall away. I do not use the word 'critic' about myself, you understand, but it is used of me, at Hounslow and elsewhere, and one cannot object.

I walked at first quickly, then more and more slowly, engaged in internal argument. A part of me wished to confirm my suspicions, a part to disprove and forget them. A part of me would be content to look at the outside of the house, to observe uncurtained windows and Meralda Forbes-Duthie going about some innocent domestic business in a front room, and to continue on its way to South Kensington Station. Another part wished to see those front windows curtained also, and perhaps shuttered, as clear evidence of nefarious goings-on. No part of me was going to enjoy knocking on the front door, yet, however slowly I might drag my feet, there was a part determined to do so. I had decided that I would represent myself as a member of the Social Democrats, compiling a register of potential supporters. Perhaps no one would answer my knock, in which case I would call again. If there were an answer, I should be turned away, but by whom?

I lingered for a while outside the house. The curtains were not drawn, but what I could see of the interior of the ground-floor room gave no indication either of villainy or its absence. Should I have provided myself with a clipboard? A canvasser for the S.D.P. would carry such a thing, and a list on it, with names to be ticked. For a moment I contemplated going away, buying a clipboard, and returning with it, but being on my way to the office, I had my briefcase, and that would have to do. Should I not first be seen to inquire at the front doors of other houses? No canvasser would have marked out Meralda Forbes-Duthie alone as a likely prospect. My cover, of which I had become rather proud as I walked to the Library, now began to seem distinctly thin.

Hesitation. A flicker at the first-floor window of the house; I had been noticed. Well, yes, I had. Further down the street, a man who had been about to get into his car had stopped, the car door open, and was gazing back at me. He wore a blue pin-striped suit with a mauve handkerchief in the top pocket, and may have been one of the infinite generation of Campbells. I knew myself to be a seeker after truth, but what the world saw was a shifty stranger with a scuffed briefcase dawdling outside a burgleable property. I must carry out my intention or give it up. I turned, breathed deeply thrice and straightened my spine so as to achieve the confident relaxation which is the promise of the Alexander Method properly applied, pushed open the iron gate of the tiny front-garden, and stepped inside. The front door of the house opened, and the old lady emerged, dressed for the street.

My mouth opened, but there was no time for my prepared question even if I had been able to form the words. I was there in her way, but she would have walked through me, if I had not stepped aside onto polyanthus. I looked up at the first-floor window, and clearly saw the younger woman looking down at me, before she stepped back into the room. The old woman was already on her way down the terrace, supported by her metal sticks, graciously inclining her head towards the man with the mauve handkerchief. Perhaps I should have rung the doorbell anyway, but I did not believe that it would be answered.

At South Kensington Station, putting coins into the automatic machine for my ticket, I found that I was flushed and a little dizzy. Had anybody pushed me, I might have fallen over, but nobody did. This feeling persisted until I was on the train, sitting as far away from other passengers as I could get, when I began to shake as if in the grip of an anxiety-attack. I wished entirely to forget the whole episode, but instead, as I held my fingers in front of my closed eyes, I could clearly see, at a distance and surrounded by a pink haze like an enduring after-image, the lighted room, the two women and the dog. It came to me then that the younger woman had been wearing white gloves, wearing them indoors, and that again, during the moment of humiliation which I had just endured, while I had seen her staring down at me, one hand at her throat, she had still been wearing them.

The list of those who have played Charley's Aunt in films

is interesting. Besides Benny (1941) and Bolger (1952 in a musical version), there was Syd Chaplin (1925; he was Charlie Chaplin's elder brother), Charles Ruggles (1931) and Arthur Askey (1940 in a version called *Charley's Big-Hearted Aunt*, which was said to have been more travesty than travestie).

VERTIGO

NEXT DAY I WAS STOPPED IN THE STREET BY THE OLD LADY.

'I have been told to ask you . . .'

'Yes?'

'You live in the house opposite?'

'Yes.'

'No more than that? You really live there? You're local?'

'You know I am. You've seen me before, here in the street. Over several years.'

'I was told to ask.'

She began to move away. I followed. 'By whom? Told by whom?'

'I think you know. Please continue your journey.'

'I was only going to the shops.'

'Please go to the shops.' She left me, and turned the corner into the Fulham Road.

It was only weekend shopping: there was not much to buy. Milk, orange-juice, eggs, bacon. I had half a loaf of bread, but it had gone mouldy, as bread usually does with me. Frozen Pasta Shells with Seafood for that Saturday night, and frozen Canelloni for the Sunday. (After my wife left, I began by making a point of cooking a regular Sunday roast, but I soon gave up.) Tea-bags, muesli. Salad—but I still had some Chinese Cabbage from the week-end before. On Mondays and Tuesdays there is often lunch, given by one of the film distributors, proper sit-down lunches at the Ivy or the Waldorf or somewhere comparable, so that I rarely eat more than breakfast at home at the beginning of the week. Wine is served at these lunches, as much as one cares to drink, but I have watched too many of my colleagues sleep through afternoon showings, and take very little.

I returned from shopping, unpacked the carrier-bag on the kitchen table, and began putting away. I looked across and down at the first-floor window opposite, which had been curtained as before when I was washing-up. The curtain had now been drawn back. Since the room was not lighted, I could not see far into it, and nothing of interest, not even the dog. It occurred to me to wonder how they would manage to exercise the dog.

The invitation to pay them a visit was made that evening by the younger woman, who may have been looking out for me. I had made tea without glancing across, but did so for a moment when I took the tea-tray back into the kitchen, and saw her sitting at the first-floor window, apparently reading a newspaper. She must have been able to see over the top of it, however, for she lowered the paper quickly, made a beckoning movement with one hand, raised the paper again, then repeated the whole sequence of movements. I nodded slowly three times. The paper remained raised, but the hand acknowledged my response.

Although I had accepted the invitation, I found that I was in two minds about going. Vague and inconclusive as the conversation that morning with the old woman had been, it had diminished the extent of·my obsession by removing from it the elements of frustration and uncertainty. I now knew that something was, in fact, up, and that my suspicions, conjectures, even my humiliating visit to the house on the day before, were, to a certain extent, justified. The question was, the extent of that extent.

For most of the day I had kept no watch on the window; if I had, I might have been beckoned over earlier. Instead I had read three of my pupils' appalling scripts, tinkered a little with Clint Eastwood, and taken my usual Saturday afternoon walk in Kensington Gardens, revolving the matter in my mind, but with no Hitchcockian urgency. On the one hand, what I had instinctively felt, that the old woman was being terrorised by the younger, had been given some confirmation; she was clearly under stress and under orders. As for the younger, though the matter of her sex remained in doubt, her wearing of gloves indoors suggested disguise, as well as the desire not to leave fingerprints. Against that, the old woman had not been murdered, nor was it likely that her murder was planned, or she would not have been encouraged to accost me. She knew and accepted her visitor, was free to leave the house (so that she could have asked for help if she believed herself to be in danger), and although she lived alone, must have occasional visitors, even if only a cleaning woman. As for the gloves, pehaps they were nothing to do with fingerprints at all, but a means of keeping the hands soft or hiding unsightly warts. If one were considering a domestic explanation for what I had seen, might not even the old lady's fear have been induced by the threat of removal from her maisonette to an Old Folks' Home?

Well, no, it must be more than that. The need to be reassured that I was local, therefore not a man put across the road to spy, indicated more than warts and the Geriatric Ward, but maybe not much more. I changed my slippers for shoes, and put on my overcoat. I remembered the hours of watching, the compulsion to find out, and the dizziness and anxiety brought on by my failure. Now that it seemed as if I were about to be given the explanation I had been seeking, I was reluctant to receive it. So much of my life was flat and anti-climactic. For a short while, unpleasant as it had mainly been, I had lived inside a movie, a stand-in miraculously allowed to play the scene, and I did not relish a return to reality.

In the event, they began by lying to me.

At close quarters, it was obvious that my instinct had been correct; the younger woman was a man. He was introduced as 'my niece, Miss Dunlop', but asked to be called Carole. Mrs Forbes-Duthie must have been well into her seventies. Any niece might be expected to be no younger than forty. Carole appeared to be in his twenties, and was, I observed, still wearing white gloves; they were of a fabric thicker than cotton, and extended well above the wrist. Naughtily I admired them, asked what they were made of, and was told that they were of kid. 'Good Lord!' I said. 'I thought kid gloves went out with the nineteenth century.' Carole replied that one could still get them if one knew where to look.

I was given sherry from a decanter into which it must have been poured several months earlier, perhaps years. Carole took a fairly hefty gulp of his, and since his expression did not change, I concluded that he was unused to sherry, and expected it to taste odd. He was nervous, I curious, Mrs Forbes-Duthie—well, it was hard to tell; most of the tension seemed to have gone out of her, leaving her resigned to what would come, though not expecting it to be pleasant. I decided that the evening would not be as flat and anti-climactic as I had feared.

I had been placed on the sofa, between the two of them, who sat in armchairs on either side of the fireplace. Carole was nervous, but not careless; he sat with his legs crossed, but below the knees, in a ladylike way. I asked to be called Paul. I said that it was so pleasant to be invited out of an evening, since I lived by myself, and seldom went out except professionally. Silence fell.

They had not asked me what my profession was. Either they knew already, or were totally uninterested in me as a person. Carole said, 'We noticed you watching.'

'I'm sorry. I couldn't help myself.'

'Then you came round to the house.'

'One gets obsessed.' Carole seemed not to understand. The old lady gave no indication either way. 'Curiosity. I was curious. I thought . . . What I'd seen seemed to be rather threatening.'

'Why?'

I turned to the old lady for support. 'I thought you were frightened. I may have been mistaken.'

'You thought I was threatening auntie?'

'Something like that.' Again to the old lady, 'Something

in your attitude, Mrs Forbes-Duthie. I had the impression that you might be in some sort of danger.'

'I would never threaten Aunt Meralda. I'm not that kind of person.'

'I said I might have been mistaken.'

'Well, you were.'

'Your aunt is clearly free to come and go. I mean, yesterday . . . and of course this morning, when she spoke to me.' I looked sideways again at the old woman, who gave me no response at all. 'If she were in any danger, she could ask for help.'

'You were looking through the window.'

'Accidentally.'

'I had to draw the curtain. You misunderstood. I'd only just arrived, you see. My aunt was upset.'

'Upset by your arrival?'

Carole realised that there was no more sherry in his glass, but the decanter was on the sideboard. Mrs Forbes-Duthie went to get it, and refilled Carole's glass. My own was still almost full. She left the decanter on the coffee-table in front of me. 'Auntie was upset,' Carole said.

'Yes.'

'I could never threaten anyone. I was in trouble. There was nobody else I could turn to. Aunt Meralda and I have always been close. When you're close, the way we are, a difference in age is no difference at all.'

'It's really nothing to do with me.'

'You were watching, but you got the wrong impression.'

'Very probably.'

'Then you came to the house. You'd been peeking across for most of the day, I can't think why. Then you came round. Naturally we thought . . .'

'That I was spying on you? Someone put up to spy on you?'

'No!' Carole became agitated. 'There's no reason for anyone to spy. It's quite simple. I needed money for my operation. I came to my aunt for help. Of course she was upset.'

17

Matters began to make a kind of sense. The sherry was truly noxious, but I needed time to think, so I made some play of sipping at it. A sex-change operation. The old lady would have been frightened, not upset. Carole had begun by threatening her in some way, so as to get the money, but then they had reached an accommodation. And the dog? A pet, much loved, and the old lady would have to look after it while Carole was in Morocco being cut. Why should they be afriad of surveillance? That piece did not fit: They had been afraid that I had actually been put up to spy on them, and had only been reassured by my being local.

'It's not something one likes to talk about, but since you've taken an interest.' Carole moved his chin forwards, and wriggled his back, in the manner of one about to make an embarrassing admission. 'I've been rather a naughty girl, I'm afraid, Paul; rather careless. I shall have to stay with auntie until it's all over and done with. It's very embarrassing, but it happens to a lot of girls. I'm sure you understand.'

'I'm not sure I do.'

'I'm pregnant; that's all. We have to get rid of it. It's a private matter.'

I looked at Carole, trying to put the idiotic impossibility of what I had heard into some kind of rational framework. He attempted to blush, and turned his head away. I put my glass down slowly on the coffee-table. The old woman said to Carole, 'He doesn't believe you.'

'I might have believed a sex-change operation.'

'Fuck!'

'I've been wondering how you manage to exercise the dog.'

'Oh, would you?'

Suddenly the atmosphere had lightened. You will have noted that I had, in fact, made no offer to exercise the dog. My remark had been no more than an expression of my continuing desire to fit pieces of the jig-saw correctly together, but Carole had read into it a concern for the animal's welfare. The English are an extraordinary people.

Being himself much concerned for the dog, what he assumed to be my own concern had brought me, as he believed, onto his side.

The dog was summoned. She was a bitch, inappropriately named Bonzo. Carole took my hand, and placed it on his arm, where there was bare skin between the top of his glove and the short sleeve of his dress. I was instructed to rub my hand against the bare skin, and did so; it was to give me a friendly scent. I extended the hand to Bonzo, who licked it. Carole said, 'If only you had a cheese-straw, she'd be your friend for life.'

Bonzo settled down between Carole and myself. She ignored the old lady. There was no antagonism between them; it was simply that their emotional paths did not cross. Carole said, 'It's so kind of you to offer. She's very good about doing her business; it's not that. We've put newspaper in a corner, and she goes out into the back-garden and squats last thing at night.' (I had missed this; they had not waited for the commercials.) 'But she needs the exercise; she's used to W A L K S.' Bonzo's head lifted sharply, but was deceived by the word's having been spelled out. 'I brought her lead, of course, but I can't take her out myself, and she's too strong for . . .' The sentence was left unfinished.

'Your aunt?'

'My grandmother.'

'If I'm to help you by taking Bonzo out for W A L K S sometimes, I think I should know more about your problem.' No reply. 'You never really expected me to believe you were pregnant?'

'I'm in trouble. There are people after me. I have to hide.'

'The police?'

The old lady said, 'Not the police. I should not protect him if it were the police.'

'Am I to continue to call him Carole?'

'Oh,' said Carole, 'Call me what you like. I'm not a bloody transvestite, if that's what you mean.'

'That will do, Gavin. Mr Hatcher is trying to be helpful.'

To me she said, 'The clothing is a disguise. My grandson is in danger; we cannot tell you more than that. If he were in trouble with the police, they would have ways of finding out that I am his grandmother, and would make enquiries here. Women's clothing would not fool them. These other people whom he has . . .' she searched for the word '. . . offended know very little of his background, and any of his friends whom they were able to question would know no more of me than they. Gavin's parents are dead. I am his only living relative. Lately we have been seldom in contact, but having nowhere else to turn, he has turned to me.'

'His offence is grave, then?'

'He has persuaded me that it may be mortal.'

'Christ!' Gavin said, *You two!* What a pair!'

I suppose that my language has become a little over-formal. It worries me sometimes; a film-reviewer should aspire to achieve a more colloquial style. Forty-five is not old. There are many journalists of my own age, not merely of the popular sort (five words to a sentence, two sentences to a paragraph) but educated people, writing for the weeklies, who nevertheless keep easily afloat in the currents of fashionable usage. If the *Radical* should decide to get rid of me, it might be because I were thought to be old-fashioned; I fear that greatly. One must be what one is. My temperament is anti-romantic, my mind analytical; my preference in both music and literature is for what is formal. Also I am much alone, and have become unused to casual conversation. Consequently—No, that is not it; that is my explanation of it, but it is not it. My wife says that I have constructed an image of myself, and am trying to climb inside it, and shut the door after me.

I said, 'You really believe these people want to kill you?'

'I know they do.'

'How long are they likely to look for you?'

Gavin bit her lip. 'I shall have to move on; I know that. I can't stay here for ever. I should have had a lot of money coming to me, but it's all gone wrong.'

The old lady said, 'He has been extremely foolish. He

tried to blackmail some people, who thought it safer to kill him. He escaped, but believes they will hunt him, at least for a while. Later it may be possible for him to escape abroad. We have not asked you for help. The intention was only to reassure you, since you seemed to suspect what was not the case, and your enquiries might have excited the attention of others. It was you who offered to exercise the dog.'

'And you? If there's danger?'

'He is my daughter's son. I must look after him.'

I said to Gavin, 'If it's not the police, and you're not afraid of leaving fingerprints, why do you wear gloves all the time?'

Slowly Gavin pulled the white kid glove off her right hand. Running all the way across the palm, and extending right across the back of the hand was a newly healed scar. It was as if someone had been trying to slice the hand in half with shears. Gavin said, 'It's a bit of a giveaway if you're in disguise.'

'Yes.' I no longer had any doubt that Gavin was in danger of death. Taking Bonzo for W A L K S seemed to be little enough to do if it would contribute even marginally to her safety. I said, 'You're not afraid I'll talk?'

Her eyes were extraordinarily blue, with dark lashes. The mouth was weak, the nose a little snub, but they were beautiful eyes. She said, 'You're not a talker, are you, Paul? You keep things in. And I want someone to know. In case anything happens.'

I found that I had an odd wivvery feeling at the pit of my stomach. I put out my hand, and touched Bonzo's head. She yawned. Gavin said, 'Bonzo likes you. That's the main thing.'

Bonzo did like me. I would have written 'did seem to like me', since I am not one who is hasty in laying claim to the liking of others, but dogs do not pretend; if they do not feel liking, they do not show it. We went for a long walk next day (Sunday), and when we had reached Kensington

Gardens and had ventured some way in, she stopped, sat down, looked up at me, and whined. She was saying that here were grass and trees, and it was usual to be allowed off the lead.

I said, 'But what if you don't come back?'

She whined again. She would come back.

She had one of those tubes attached to her collar, which are used to contain an owner's name, address and telephone number, and perhaps the promise of a reward, but they would be the address and telephone number from which Gavin had fled, and of no use in reuniting them if she were to be lost.

I said, 'I dare not.'

Again she raised her head and gazed directly at me, then lifted one paw and placed it on the hand which held her leash. I felt that same wivvery feeling in the stomach as I had when looking into Gavin's eyes the evening before. I had become, you see, so very unused to any direct relationship: it is easy to upset the emotionally detached. I let her off the lead. She bounded away from me; she was like a gazelle. No, she was like what she was, a dog of the chase. She barked. She ran back to me, reassuring me, and then was off again. There was a small child in a light blue woollie, running before its mother towards the Round Pond. I thought, 'Dear God! That small child is prey to her. She will savage it.' Bonzo ignored the small child. She ran, jumped, spun in the air, snuffled at enticing scents, pissed on the Peter Pan statue, shat shamelessly where nannies might walk in it, returning always to frolic at my feet, and when it was time to leave the Gardens, and I stood and called 'Bonzo!' holding out the lead, she came at once, stood quite still while I attached the leash to her collar, and walked with me sedately down the Gloucester Road, right along the Cromwell Road, left into the Earls Court Road where the windows of the food shops were piled high with samosas, and so left again into the Old Brompton Road and on home. I was tempted to bring her into the flat to take tea with me, but it would have been a liberty, when she was not my dog.

Mrs Forbes-Duthie opened the door to me. 'Thank you. I shan't ask you in.'

I said, 'I really enjoyed it. I'm working all day tomorrow, but I'll come in the evening.' I let Bonzo off the lead, and she licked my hand, and went indoors.

Seated on the wicker sofa in my study, eating heated-up cannelloni, still in its foil container, from a tray, I watched *Mastermind* on television that night. One of the contestants had chosen *The British Film Industry, 1900–1930* as his Special Subject. 'Who was the English playwright who provided the story-idea for the first feature film made in Britain by the Famous Players—Lasky Company?' Since the question was one I had myself supplied, I knew the answer, though the contestant, who had clearly made a foolish choice of subject, did not. 'Henry Arthur Jones,' I said aloud, but there was no one to hear and applaud me.

Bonzo and I took a short turn with the leash to Chelsea Green on the Monday evening, and round Onslow Square on the Tuesday. On Wednesday, Thursday and Friday afternoons, we went for proper walks. Already by Thursday, Bonzo herself came to the door when I rang the bell, and scratched for it to be opened. I began to feel guilty that she should show such open affection towards me in the presence of her owner, and suggested that Gavin might like to accompany us on the Saturday afternoon, well wrapped up and with a veil. The invitation was declined.

The friendship between Bonzo and myself ripened through all that week and the next. Within the house, I was entertained once more to the terrible sherry (and was glad to see the end of the decanter), but the conversation did not flow. Gavin did not wish to talk about her predicament, but clearly thought of little else. She had taken to hiding her blue eyes behind dark glasses, and to lying long abed, perhaps to save wear and tear on her wardrobe, which could not easily be replaced by Mrs Forbes-Duthie, who was of a smaller size. It had been thought prudent that she should appear briefly to the cleaning lady in her character as niece, but as a martyr to migraine, stretched out on the sofa with the curtains drawn, and the cleaning lady had hoovered respectfully round her.

'I shall have to move on,' she said, 'I know I shall. I can't stay here much longer. It's not fair to anyone.'

'I suppose there's no way of reassuring these people, whoever they are, that you're no longer a danger to them? I take it you've given up the idea of blackmail. If they knew that, they might decide to leave you alone.'

'I bit off more than I could chew; that's the truth of it. I must have that dog put down, and go abroad.' I thought my heart would stop. Yet if I had wanted a dog, I could long ago have been to the Battersea Lost Dogs Home, and found one. Gavin said, 'Only I haven't any money, and I don't know how I could get a passport, dressed up like this.'

At two o'clock on the Saturday morning, my telephone rang briefly, waking me, but ceasing to ring before I could answer. Woken thus abruptly, one wakes as if from a nightmare, which persists into the period of waking. *Silence that dreadful bell. It frights the isle/From her propriety.* The bell was already silent, but South Kensington had begun to be frighted; there was disturbance across the gardens. The phone! Nobody phoned me, particularly at night. I got out of bed quickly, and went to the bedroom window. On every floor of the houses of the terrace opposite, lights were being switched on. There was an indefinite shouting, screaming, banging, which, when I opened the window, became louder but no more definite. I dressed quickly, and ran downstairs to the ground-floor flat, leaving my own door on the latch.

I banged on the door. The tenants were Australians, already wakeful; perhaps they had not yet gone to bed. I said, 'May I go into your garden?' and went on quickly past them, through the living-room and out of the French window, they following. I don't know what I expected to do. I had been summoned; I was sure of that; the telephone had summoned me, but the summons had been interrupted. Perhaps I had some vague idea of climbing the wall between the two gardens, and entering Mrs Forbes-Duthie's maisonette from the back. I, who have watched two black teenagers beating up a drunk on a platform of the London Underground, and not interfered, had some such notion of arriving in the nick of time like the U.S. Cavalry to the rescue of Gavin and her grandmother.

I could have phoned the police? Why had I not phoned the police? But others would by now have done so.

So many lights were shining from the houses on both sides that the gardens were partially lit. Vague noises came from those houses, a susurration of concern below the mixture of noises coming from Number 12, which now resolved themselves into the most definite and prolonged scream of pain. The crash of broken glass. From that very first-floor window in which I had first seen them framed only a fortnight ago, the old woman, the younger woman and the dog, a body fell into a flower-bed. No, it had not fallen, but had flung itself through the window, the dog leaping behind it, and now picked itself up, looking wildly from side to side, while at the broken window above, a dark figure appeared, and then turned to run downstairs.

I shouted. I did not shout, 'Gavin!' I did nothing to help Gavin at all. I shouted, 'Bonzo!' and the dog came to me, leaping over the dividing wall as easily as through the broken window.

One cannot hurl oneself through a window without sustaining injury. Gavin must have been bleeding from the face and arms at least. There was light in the garden, but not enough to allow me to distinguish such details. I could see that he had lost his wig; there was a man's head above the dress. He began to climb the drainpipe which ran up the side of the house. It was not a way to escape. I do not think he can have intended any escape from those who hunted him except into a quick death. He could have run across the garden, and been over the low wall before they caught him. He would then have been in the company of law-abiding

25

strangers, of rate-payers of the Royal Borough, and it would not have been easy to molest or abduct him. But he did not choose that way. Instead he climbed.

The white gloves went up and up, one hand above the other. One could see only them; the white face was certainly obscured by blood, and the body was a dark shape below. But the white gloves climbed. They reached the level of the first floor, then the second, then the third. Men had come out of the Forbes-Duthie maisonette and into the garden, but no notice was taken of them at that time. They were looking upwards at the white gloves, as were we all.

The white gloves had reached the roof, and as Gavin followed them on to it, his whole body could clearly be seen against the never-dark night-sky of Central London. He looked down, hesitated, then jumped. There was crazy-paving beyond the flower-bed, and he aimed for that. Because of the low wall between, I did not see him strike it, but the sound was as of a melon bursting. One of those who watched from windows began to sob. It was from our terrace; there was no sign anywhere of Mrs Forbes-Duthie. The men in the garden picked up Gavin's body, and carried it indoors. They were wearing police-uniforms. I went back indoors, taking Bonzo with me.

THE MAN WHO
KNEW TOO MUCH

GAVIN HAD DIED WHILE ATTEMPTING TO ESCAPE ARREST. HE
was a bisexual transvestite, who had battered his grandmother to death before the police broke into the house.

I knew that this could not be true. As far as one could tell,
Gavin had been fond of his grandmother, and she of him; in
trouble, he had turned to her. He had no reason to batter her.
Also I was bothered by the words of the announcement,
which seemed to suggest that *because* he was a bisexual
transvestite (and therefore mentally disturbed), he had
murdered the old lady. But even I, with no more than an
educated layman's knowledge, knew that to be bisexual
and/or transvestite (the two not necessarily going together)
is not to be mad in any clinical sense, though one may
become depressed, as any human may, by the inconvenience of one's own condition. Nor do transvestites incline to
battery. Finally, since neither transvestism or bisexuality is
any longer illegal, the police had no right in law to break
into Mrs Forbes-Duthie's maisonette, since, even if Gavin
had battered his grandmother, they could not have known
that until they had already gained entry. I thought these
thoughts, but I did not speak them aloud.

In my mind's eye, I saw her, the old lady, her face
battered, her head beaten in. There had been scratches on
the face of one of the policemen who had carried Gavin's
body indoors; I had seen his face clearly in the light from
the room as he had entered by the French window. He might
have received those scratches from Gavin, except that if

27

Gavin had been so close, how had he managed to get away from four policemen? Bonzo might have bitten the policeman in defending her master, but these were not incapacitating bites, merely scratches. In my mind's eye I saw her, the old lady, as fierce and foolish as an old scrawny cat, fighting for her kitten, and I saw the policeman, growing finally impatient, batter in her head.

I write 'the policeman'. Should I not write, 'the man in police-uniform'? But it was the police who informed the news-media that Gavin had died while attempting to escape arrest. The announcement was reported on the radio that day and in the newspapers on Sunday. Surprisingly, it was given no great prominence, even in the popular papers. There were no photographs of the house and garden with superimposed cross or circle to mark the spot where the body struck the crazy-paving, and it was clear that the police had released (and the papers accepted and printed) only one photograph of Gavin, a conventional head-and-shoulders studio portrait which, I assumed, they had discovered among his grandmother's effects. The cleaning-lady had been interviewed. She had noticed nothing remarkable about Mrs Forbes-Duthie's 'niece' beyond the fact that she had been ill with her nerves and required rest and quiet; it was, and had always been, a quiet house, and the old lady a very kind and thoughtful person, though often in pain from arthritis. A friend of Gavin, Damian something-or-other, an interior decorator, told reporters that Gavin had been a very private person, artistic in his tastes, had enjoyed music and theatre, did sometimes go to 'clubs', but preferred a quiet life: —'quiet' was a word which seemed to crop up in every context. Gavin had lived alone in a flat of two rooms, with kitchenette and bathroom, in a mansion block near Primrose Hill, and had worked in some junior capacity in the Television Department of an advertising agency, where he had been well-liked by all with whom he worked, but intimate with none of them.

The Monday newspapers printed the story on their inside pages with no significant additions. By Wednesday it had ceased to be mentioned. There must have been an inquest, but it was not reported. When one considers the melodramatic and violent nature of what had happened, the response of the news-media seemed strangely muted. Quiet, in fact.

I had returned to my own flat with Bonzo, as has been recorded, where I spent some time picking small splinters of glass from her chest and front legs, and applying pine disinfectant to the wounds. Then I went back to bed. Bonzo slept on the end of it, and weighed heavily on my legs. We slept late. During the day, I extended my weekend shopping by the purchase of a large dog-basket, a blanket, dishes for food and water, and a leash: I did not feel able to claim the old one from the house opposite, where the police could be seen to be in occupation.

During that weekend, though of course I was curious, as all my neighbours must also have been, I did not often look across and down into the Forbes-Duthie windows, because I did not dare to be seen to be taking interest. But I did look sometimes, when I thought it might be natural to do so, and then I looked for the policeman with the scratched face, but did not see him. I continued to think my own thoughts, but no Hitchcockian curiosity now could lead me into investigation and involvement. Of the original three framed in that window, the old woman and the younger were already dead, and my responsibility, as it seemed to me, was to no abstract search for truth, but to the living dog, Bonzo.

The police phoned inconveniently on the Monday to say that they wished to interview me. I was on my way downstairs, already late for a Press Show at the Odeon, Leicester Square, but, as I have remarked, my telephone does not often ring, so I ran back up half a flight and unlocked the double-locked door to answer it. I had spent time explaining to Bonzo that she would be alone all day, but that I should return in the evening, and that I should have to confine her to the kitchen until I could be sure that she would not chew furniture in my absence. I heard her barking as I opened the door, as if to say, 'How swiftly time passes!' Consequently I was a little tetchy with the police, and told them flatly that, owing to the demands of my profession, I should be unable to call at Chelsea Police Station until the Wednesday afternoon. The sergeant who was phoning received this equably, and suggested that Thursday morning might be even more convenient for me; it was only a matter of taking statements from everyone who had witnessed the incident, and meanwhile perhaps I would like to jot down a few notes by way of preparation. I said I would come on Wednesday afternoon, and rang off.

The question was how much to tell them. It would be prudent not to know too much. That the police version of what had occurred could not be true, I was sure; that they themselves had killed the old lady (for whatever reason), I suspected. Gavin had said that those who hunted him were not the police, yet they were four policemen who had burst into the house at two a.m. To inform the police that Gavin feared for his life might lead me into a situation in which I had reason to fear for my own. Yet there was the dog, which had run to me across two gardens, and remained with me. That could not have escaped notice; the Australians at least would have noticed it, and, when interviewed have mentioned it. I decided to own to the dog.

At the Chelsea Police Station, there is a large entrance hall, across which runs a counter, dividing the police from the public; I find this symbolic. One presents oneself to the Desk Sergeant, who presides behind the counter, and states one's business first to him. I had expected to be taken to an office, but was instead conducted to the Interview Room which is to one side of the counter. Entry to it is by two doors, one from the police side, one from the public. I entered by the public door, escorted by a constable, who left me there to wait, closing the door after him. I do not say he locked it, but he closed it firmly, and I had the impression that he remained outside.

The walls were bare, with no windows, the floor of

composition tiles, uncarpeted. The light was artifical from a
central fitting, and the air must have been filtered in from
outside. There was a wooden table in the middle of the
room, and two straight wooden chairs, one on each side of
it; two other similar chairs had been set against a wall. The
ceiling was a smoke-stained cream, the walls brown; there
were two radiators, also painted brown, the composition
tiles of the floor were a darker brown. There were no
armchairs, no magazines, not even the *Police Gazette*.
There was a cheap metal ash-tray on the table. The intention
of such a room is, I imagine, to induce, even in respectable
people, feelings of criminality.

I sat on one of the chairs against the wall, and waited.
After ten minutes, a uniformed inspector entered the room
from the police side, followed by a man in a brown suit. To
my own inward fury, I found myself standing up as they
entered. 'Please!' said the inspector, and indicated the chair
by the table. 'I'm sorry to have kept you waiting. Mr
Hatcher, isn't it?' I sat, and he sat at the table opposite me,
placing a file of documents and a blank pad of A4 lined
paper in front of him. The inspector introduced neither
himself nor the man in the brown suit, who moved one of
the straight chairs from where it had been set to a place
about two feet behind and to one side of the inspector's
chair, and sat there, watching and listening. The inspector
took a fountain pen from the top pocket of his uniform
jacket, and unscrewed it carefully.

I said, 'I think I should tell you straight away about the
dog.'

'Ah, yes. May I just have your full name?' I gave it.
'And the address?'

They must have known my full name; they must have
known my address. It is all done to unsettle one.

'And you work as a journalist for . . ?' He consulted the
file and made a note. 'Yes. Now what can we do for you,
Mr Hatcher?'

'You asked me to come here.'

'You wanted to say something about a dog?'

31

I was by then unsettled. 'I was asked to exercise the dog by Mrs Forbes-Duthie's niece.'

'Niece?'

'I thought she was his niece—*he* was *her* niece.' They were both looking at me patiently. I was sweating; they would be able to smell the sweat. 'I didn't know that the person to whom Mrs Forbes-Duthie introduced me as her niece—that is, the person she introduced *as* her niece to me—I didn't know that this person was, in fact, a man.'

'A man?'

'That's what the papers say.'

'Were you a friend of Mrs Forbes-Duthie?'

'A neighbour. I'd seen her in the street from time to time. She approached me just a fortnight ago. In the street.'

'And asked you to exercise her niece's dog?'

'Invited me for a glass of sherry. It was the niece who asked me to exercise the dog. She wasn't well, she said. The dog needed exercise, and was too strong for her aunt.'

'The dog was more used to a man?'

'She didn't say so.'

'*She* didn't?'

'She, as I thought.'

'Why should they choose you, do you think?'

'One can't tell. Mrs Forbes-Duthie may have known that I live alone. I don't know how, but these matters *are* known; one talks to the caretaker if one has a problem. A divorced man in middle age, living alone—she may have thought me suitable.'

'To meet her niece?'

'To exercise the dog. People do things on impulse; one can't tell why. You'd have to ask her, except—'

'Except that she can't tell us either. The cremation's on Saturday, if you were thinking of going. Wimbledon.' A note made. 'And you agreed to exercise the dog?'

'Once. Then I found I quite enjoyed it. I usually do walk in the park of a week-end, and the dog was company. As a matter of fact, I've grown quite fond of the dog. Obviously, if anyone else should have any claim on her, any legal claim, I have none. Except affection.'

'Oh, I don't think anyone's bothered about the dog. You really never noticed that the niece was a transvestite?'

'She wore dark glasses. She was dressed as a woman, spoke as a woman, was introduced to me as a woman. I've seen Mrs Forbes-Duthie around the neighbourhood for years. One wouldn't suspect such deception. And after that first occasion, I hardly met the niece. The dog used to scratch at the other side of the front door when I rang the bell.'

'And Mrs Forbes-Duthie? Did she seem . . ?'

'In no way out of the ordinary.' My voice came out rather firmer than I had intended, but seemed to convince him.

'The ground-floor tenants of your building say that, on the night of the incident, you knocked at their door and demanded to be let into the garden.'

I had prepared myself for this. 'I could hear the noises opposite. I was concerned.'

'For Mrs Forbes-Duthie?'

'For the dog.'

Another note. 'The dog.' He looked up. 'Well, that's understandable. Clearly you're fond of the dog.' He read back through his notes. 'Is there anything else you want to tell me about your visit to the house?' There was nothing. 'Nothing odd you can remember? Nothing said, nothing done?' Nothing. 'Would you mind describing for me what you saw from the garden on the night of the incident?' I described. The inspector made notes. 'Four policemen, you say? Did you see them at all clearly? Is there anything you remember particularly about them?'

For a moment I considered carrying the war into the enemy's camp by telling him that one of the policemen had a scratched face, but I thought better of it. 'I wasn't looking at them. I was watching the man in the dress, climbing.'

'The niece?'

'I never really noticed the policemen. They carried the

body indoors, I think, but by that time my attention was on the dog.'

Then suddenly it was over. 'Thank you very much, Mr Hatcher. If we need to see you again, we'll give you good notice.'

'Do I have to sign anything?'

'Oh, I shouldn't think so.' He picked up the file, and stood. I stood also, hesitant, then turned towards the door. The man in the brown suit, who had remained sitting, said, 'Why did you visit the house on the morning before she spoke to you?'

The world stopped. When Joshua fought the battle of Jericho, he blew his horn, the world ceased to revolve, and the walls of the city fell over. The man in the brown suit, silent up to then, had blown his horn, and my walls fell over. As long as the world revolves, one is not conscious of its movement; only when it has stopped spinning does it seem to spin. My world was spinning. The man in the brown suit said, 'Something the matter?'

'No.'

'I asked you a question. Why did you call at the house on the Friday morning?'

'It was the dog.'

The man in the brown suit said, 'It's always the bloody dog with you.'

The inspector returned to his place at the table, flipped open the pad, and unscrewed the top of his pen again. This time he did not ask me to sit also. I said, 'I'm sorry you should believe I have concealed anything. It didn't seem to be of any importance, and since I was embarrassed by the incident, I didn't mention it.'

The man in the brown suit said, 'You tell us what happened. We'll decide if it's important.'

The day was chilly, being the first of December, and the wind from the north-east. Nevertheless I felt sweat trickle from my crotch down the inside of my leg. All my senses preternaturally sharp at that moment of, as it seemed to me, positive danger, I marked the progress of profuse perspiration from my armpit down my inner arm, and heard each several drop in succession strike the composition tiles of the floor. Only under the influence of cannabis (a rare experience for me, since I do not smoke, and have to chew the nasty stuff) have my senses functioned at such a pitch. Yet I was calm. I knew that I must tell the truth insofar as I might with prudence do so; I should only trap myself by invention. I explained that I had looked through the window, and seen the two women with Bonzo. I had known nothing of the docility and friendliness of Bonzo's true nature, only that an old lady, whom I knew to live alone and had often seen at that window before, seemed now to be confronted in her own home by a savage alsatian. I had thought her frightened of the dog, had spent all day brooding on the matter, and by the Friday morning had decided where my duty lay. I had called at the house to offer assistance, only to meet the old lady on her way to the shops, and manifestly in no need of my help. I had been confused, confounded, embarrassed, had retreated without explanation. On the Saturday, Mrs Forbes-Duthie had herself approached me in the street, had received my stumbling explanation of my behaviour, and had issued her invitation to meet Bonzo for myself over sherry.

It was not bad, by no means bad, when one considers that it was all on the spur of the moment, and while still in a state of shock. It convinced them. There were further questions about Gavin, about the old lady, about what exactly had been said, about what I had noticed, particularly in regard to Gavin. 'A very charming gentle person,' I said, and the inspector said, 'They're like that, aren't they? Devious! I expect he fancied you.'

It became clear that we were covering ground already well covered. The inspector ceased to make notes, and my confidence returned. 'That's really all I can tell you,' I said. 'I hardly saw the niece, and our conversation was almost entirely about the dog.'

This time it was the man in the brown suit who stood up. 'Alright! You can piss off.'

The uniformed inspector said, 'Thank you so much, Mr Hatcher, for assisting us with our enquiries.'

My wife has become a televison personality. That is how the rot set in; it is hard to be married to a public person. When first we met she was what is called a 'researcher', a lowly class of person in television terms, although usually recruited from the university-educated. She was employed by the B.B.C. on one of those programmes about films which are a staple of public-service broadcasting: the title may change, but not the format. For half an hour fortnightly between September and March, a 'presenter' of indeterminate age, usually dressed in the kind of casual clothes which were fashionable five years earlier, introduces clips from current releases: there will also be an interview with some director or leading actor on location, and perhaps a quiz. The presenter's introductions are not reviews, since they are too short to allow analysis and must include a summary of the plot. They will, however, be flippant in tone, knowing, and often dismissive, so as to establish the intellectual superiority of the presenter to what he presents, as well as the independence of the B.B.C. itself from the commercial interests of the distributors who are providing the clips (adding up to at least fifteen minutes of programme-time) for nothing:—the B.B.C. has, since it began, created more varieties of intellectual dishonesty than the church and the universities put together.

Those who review films professionally have been found unsuitable to present such programmes, but in the early days, the producers of B.B.C. Television's Arts and Features did not know this, so that some of us were tested, and found wanting. Back in the sixties, when I was in my twenties, and was at the beginning of what now, I suppose with hindsight, could hardly be called a career (since a career assumes progress, and I have made none), I was one of those tested. I did not get to appear in front of a camera; I failed the lunch. But I did get to meet Anne, who had read

36

English at Oxford, as I did, but four years after me, so that our paths never crossed there.

I was young. I was, as Graham Greene had been in the thirties, the film critic of an important weekly journal of opinion. The circulation of the *Radical* then was twice what it is today. I could not know that it was on the downward slope, its Fabian readers dying off or succumbing to senile dementia, its politics of decency and common-sense increasingly outmoded. I could not know that I would never finish my novel, was not, as Graham Greene was, a taster of new experience, an inventor, a mover-on, but merely a conscientious and obsessed reviewer of other people's work, a barnacle which had put out its curly tendrils to test the surface on which it found itself, and did not know that they were already hardening into calcium.

I could not know this: Anne did not. Like most people of her age, she assumed in those close to her the qualities she had herself. We liked each other, had read many of the same books, enjoyed movies, made each other laugh. I must have seemed confident, must have believed that I was on the way up; we would make the climb together. At first one of us would spend the night in the other's flat because it was too far to go home, then we would pass week-ends together either at Hampstead or Holland Park—the Sunday papers in bed, with croissants and proper coffee, sex again before rising, and a movie or a walk on the Heath or in the Park during the afternoon. Finally we looked for somewhere to live together, and so drifted into marriage, enjoyed that comfortable state for ten years, endured it for five, and drifted this time into divorce.

Anne was not beautiful, but she had a quality which is more attractive than beauty; she had concern. Those who lived with her (her mother, I myself), knew that this concern was instant; it could be transferred within seconds from one person or cause to another. I do not mean to suggest that my wife's concern was not genuine; she had a genuine concern to solve immediate problems. Those problems which were not swiftly soluble, or which were merely the symptoms of some deeper malaise, did not hold her interest; she must have results, and settled for symptomatic relief. Her temperament and gifts were uniquely suitable for television.

She had moved, soon after we married, from researching films to a programme which championed ordinary members of the public against those who would exploit, cheat, manipulate or simply ride smoothshod over them. The presenter, who had himself brought the idea to the B.B.C., was a middle-aged actor who had specialised in playing probation officers, the editors of local newspapers and compassionate clergymen, and who liked to be known as 'the English Spencer Tracy'. His idea had found an immediate public response. A thirteen-week series had been followed by others of twenty-six. Weekly, with a mixture of high-minded indignation and throwaway wit, he exposed corrupt mail-order operators, fly-by-night builders, estate-agents who sold non-existent villas in Lindos and the Algarve to pensioners, heartless officialdom, hospital boards which covered-up the amputations of limbs from patients who only required dentistry, dilatory and defaulting solicitors, sellers of outdated encyclopaedias from door to door and the monsters who employed them, rogue computers, unqualified and even disqualified tree-surgeons; the list was limitless. Anne joined the team of researchers who sorted through viewers' letters for suitable examples of injustice and negligence, and would sally out weekly on missions of investigation and confrontation, with no more by way of protection against enraged villains than the producer and his P.A., sound and camera crews, a driver and (on a dull day) perhaps a couple of electricians. Film of these encounters would be inserted into the programme, which was otherwise live, and Anne would be seen on this film, and sometimes she was allowed to make her own report before the studio audience. She was reasonably photogenic, an Oxbridge version of the girl next door; she was always assured, and she had concern. In her third year with the programme, she became assistant-presenter. At the end of the fourth, when the Enlgish Spencer Tracy had offended his masters at the B.B.C. unforgiveably by making a commerical for pet-food, she was promoted to presenter.

On the Thursday afternoon, when I returned from my walk with Bonzo, I found on the table in the hall downstairs an envelope delivered by hand from the B.B.C. Television Centre which contained a card of invitation to Anne's show that night. Though the programme was no longer transmitted live, it was still performed to a studio audience, recorded on a Thursday to be put out on Saturday. I had not been physically present at a performance for ten years, had not even watched it on television. Yet the invitation could only have been sent by my wife herself, who never did anything without sound reason.

Bonzo had already shown that she could be left. I decided that I had better obey what could only be a summons.

I arrived, was admitted with the rest of the studio audience, and took a seat high at the back where I was least likely to be shown on camera. The show, I noticed, had lightened in character; there was more whimsicality and less investigative reporting. A small group, seated at the front, had brought in mynah birds, which were set to reciting *The Road to Mandalay* in competition with each other. One of the birds could not recite at all, but entranced the audience by repeating, 'Silly old sod!' *ad infinitum*, and was awarded a Special Prize by my wife. Flat-dwellers in Gateshead, all unemployed, had complained that they suffered from persistent damp and falling masonry, which the council would do nothing to ameliorate, but instead of a filmed investigation, we had the whole story put wittily into song by a young man in a crimson dinner-jacket. Another gentleman read *risqué* misprints from the small adds in *The Times*. There was only one *exposé* proper, where once there would have been half a dozen, but throughout the programme my wife radiated concern, and since it was so abundantly clear that she cared, nobody cared what she cared about. Finally the whole troupe led the audience in a caring song, the words of which were written out, as at the

Christmas pantomimes of my youth, on a sheet which descended from the studio roof, whereafter we all proceeded to the Hospitality Room for mulled wine and sausage rolls.

I said, 'It's some time since I've seen the show. It seems to have changed.'

'Yes. Gutless. The punters prefer that. And the Corporation too, of course. Less danger of being sued, and anyway it's so much cheaper. Costs a lot to send a unit out these days, particularly since the unions have toughened up on manning levels. What, send twenty people three hundred miles just to film a lot of rotting floorboards and mouldy walls and kids with rickets? We do it all with stills and funny voices nowadays, and a poof at the piano. Did you know that the incidence of tuberculosis up there has tripled in the last four years?'

My wife would never have referred to her audience as 'punters' in the old days. It is a word used by bookmakers, prostitutes, the owners of strip-clubs and sex-shops, and by the very confidence tricksters whom she had made it her business to expose. They use it of those whom it is their trade to exploit, and for whom they have no respect.

'You don't sound too happy in your work.'

'It's a living. Have you decided to change your job?'

'No. Why do you ask?'

'Snoopers. I thought maybe you were being positively vetted.'

The B.B.C.'s sausage rolls are of a special integrity; they are intended to provide nourishment without giving pleasure. I knew this, but had forgotten it, and bit into one. Looking about for somewhere to put the unconsumed portion, I remembered Bonzo, and pocketed it instead, watched by my wife. 'Are you going eccentric?' she said.

'Dog at home. Why should anyone be vetting me?'

'You tell me. I thought you should know. Why else do you think I sent you the invitation for tonight?'

'You could have phoned.'

'Thought you might be tapped.'

'Christ!' I took another sausage roll, and my wife

removed it from my hand, and put it back on the plate. Why do I write 'my wife', when I could write 'Anne'? *Anne* took the sausage roll from me—Anne, my ex-wife.

'What dog?'

'I'll tell you about the dog. You tell me about the vetting.'

It had begun with a phone-call. An educated voice. At first she had thought he was trying to sell insurance. But he was working, he said, for a government department (which one was not specified.) Would she object to answering a few questions? She had thought it was something to do with the programme, that maybe they had brought themselves into conflict somehow with the Official Secrets Act, and she had referred him to the Legal Department, but no; it was a private matter. Would she object if he were to visit her at home?'

'When?'

'Yesterday.'

He had arrived, exactly on time, well-spoken and polite. She had intended to ask him for identification, but had discovered that she lacked the confidence to do so. She excused herself to me for this lapse on the grounds that years of experience as an investigative reporter had taught her how to spot a fake, and he was clearly not a fake.

'Was he wearing a brown suit, by any chance?'

'No, I don't think so. More town and country—sort of Harris tweed jacket and cavalry twill: I can't remember. Somebody had scratched his face; that was the only remarkable aspect of his appearance.'

'Oh God!' I closed my eyes, and felt the mulled wine stir uneasily within me, as if some frightful creature were about to emerge from its depths.

'Then the questions were all about you. Politics. Money. Sexual habits. I said, "My dear man, he's a film-critic. He hasn't got any politics *or* money *or* sexual habits. Ask him yourself," and he said somebody would do that, but it was routine to question all those who knew the subject intimately. So then I asked if you were being vetted for a job, and he

41

said, "More or less." I gave him a cup of coffee, and he took three sugars. I thought you ought to know.'

'But you didn't want to phone because you thought my phone might be tapped.'

'You don't want a job; you never have, in security or anything else.'

'No.'

'What have you got yourself into, Paul? I mean, you're not Anthony Blunt either. You've never had access to anything more secret than the Library of the British Film Institute.'

'I'm certainly not a spy.'

We had wedged ourselves into a corner between the buffet and the side wall, but members of the public hung about at the edges of our privacy, waiting for the chance to tell my wife that she was doing a great job. It was neither the time nor place for confidences. I took a grip on common sense. By accident I had acquired a small piece of knowledge; I knew that Gavin had tried to blackmail someone, but not whom or how. Unfortunately the 'whom' did not know how little I knew, only that I might know something, and consequently, although not dangerous, I was myself in danger. It would be both foolish and selfish to involve Anne. I must keep quiet, keep my head down, and trust that what I had told the police would be believed.

I said, 'Look, your fans are waiting for you. Thanks a lot. If anything comes of all this, I'll let you know.'

'Are you in trouble, Paul?'

'I hope not. I'll let you know.'

'What was that about a dog?'

'Somebody gave me an alsatian. I'm getting rather fond of it.' I held out my hand, and my wife advanced her cheek to be kissed. People in the entertainment industry do kiss each other a great deal; it means nothing. I kissed Anne under the approving gaze of three mynah-bird-owners, and squeezed her hand. As I moved away, a teenage girl asked, 'Hey, Mister! Are you famous?'

'Not really,' I said. 'But I'm working on it.'

As was now usual, Bonzo slept on the end of my bed. She had done so since the night she had come to me, nearly a week before, and since mine is a three-quarter bed from the time when Anne and I slept in it together, it had been possible to work out an arrangement by which she did not weigh too heavily on my legs. I found her company comforting. Yet Bonzo had not protected Gavin. Would she protect me, if people were to come in the night?'

I got up, and double-locked my front door from the inside. My mind was a poor thing; if allowed, it would run uselessly about, like a mouse in a maze. I relaxed the muscles of my neck and shoulders, and breathed deeply. Again I summoned Common Sense, wise director of frightened mice, reassurer, giver of rest of the sleepless. Whatever enquires were made and by whomever, I could only be revealed as a very ordinary law-abiding person, complicit to no plots, unpolitical and sexually straight up-and-down. Even if the man with the scratched face were not a policeman or security agent but the emissary of some unscrupulous criminal, or even if he were a policeman, and the police were in some outrageous way party to the hounding of Gavin and the murder of his grandmother, as I myself suspected, it made no difference; the more rigorously he enquired, the more harmless I should be seen to be. Reassured at last, I fell asleep without the aid of herbal Relaxation Tablets from the Health Food Shop, and awoke refreshed.

I ate an apple, and sipped tea in the kitchen, with Bonzo's paw on my knee; she was waiting for the core. The day lay uncomplicatedly ahead of me. I would pull trousers and a polo-neck over my pyjamas, to take Bonzo round the square. No washing-up to speak of. A bath, coffee, a little shopping. Some work on Clint Eastwood, and a can of Slimline Tomato Soup for lunch. Then a walk in Kensington Gardens with Bonzo, tea for us both, and preparation for my class at Hounslow that evening, when Bonzo would have to be left in the flat. Although it was Friday, my usual journey to the office hardly seemed worthwhile. I would buy a copy of the *Radical* at the corner newsagent's.

It occurred to me that I ought to substitute my own name and address for Gavin's in the little tube which was attached to Bonzo's collar. I would not read the address when I took it out; it would be wiser to have no knowledge of Gavin's past at all; I would burn the little roll of paper, and run the ashes away down the sink. Thereafter, if Bonzo should ever stray (which Heaven forfend), she would be returned to me. I decided to offer a reward of £100. I wrote Bonzo's name and my own name, address and phone number on a quarter-sheet of writing-paper, rolled it up, and prepared to substitute it for what was in the tube already.

What was in the tube, however, was not Gavin's address at all, but a small roll of photographic negative, protected by transparent paper. There seemed to be six photographs, each about half an inch square in size. It would, of course, still have been possible to burn the negative, and dispose of the ashes. Instead, I unrolled the strip of film, and held it up to the light. Each of the photographs was of several people engaged in some joint activity, but they had been taken from a distance, so that the detail was too small to be made out; one would not be able to tell who the people were and what they were doing, without enlarging the picture, even if one had more skill than I in reading negatives.

Bonzo whined, reminding me that she would have to be taken out if she were not to disgrace herself indoors. I rolled the strip of film up again in its paper. Then, since I could think of nothing better at that time to do with it, I put it back in the tube attached to Bonzo's collar.

BLACKMAIL

A WEEK LATER, I BOUGHT MYSELF A PAPERBACK COPY OF *The Photographer's Handbook*.

You think me foolish, even mad? I had been ready to destroy a paper with Gavin's address, yet kept in my possession this far more dangerous piece of evidence. Two people, to my knowledge, had died because of it, and there might be others outside my knowledge. It looked like film (which touched on my own obsession), but was more probably part of a roll of still photographs, taken with some sort of miniature camera. They would show—my imagination could not make concrete what they would show, but whatever it was, it must be horribly compromising to some very powerful person.

Therefore the film was, in the right hands, of great value. How could one destroy something so valuable? It would be like burning money. But a valuable object has no value unless that value can be realised. Gavin had not been able to realise it, and I certainly could not, and would not, even if I could: I am not a blackmailer. The thing was not only valueless, but dangerous, and I must be rid of it. Set a match to it, and it would take fire in, quite literally, a flash.

Yet I could not follow that prudent course, which would have made nothing of two deaths. *Oh, vengeance! vengeance!* I lay awake, while Bonzo snored. The train of thought went round and round in my mind as if on the Inner Circle. It stopped at stations, the same stations, Bayswater, Paddington, Edgware Road, Baker Street, Great Portland Street, King's Cross, the same passengers got on and off, the pneumatic doors breathed heavily open and rattled shut, I sipped at orange juice and listened to the all-night buses until at last grey light replaced the dark behind the window-curtains, and I could hear the *clip! clop!* of troopers' horses in the Fulham Road.

Oh, vengeance! What were Gavin and his grandmother to me that I should avenge them?—an incompetent blackmailer and one of those Kensington widows who turn out assiduously every polling day to give the Royal Borough one of the safest Tory majorities in Britain. Objectively viewed, they were not admirable people, and their deaths did not greatly diminish the sum of human virtue. Even so, to avenge them in some legal way was my clear duty, since the murderers of old ladies should be exposed and apprehended, lest they develop a taste for it. Exposed, yes; apprehended, yes, and then confined, but by those legally empowered to do it, *videlicet* the police, to whom any information should be laid and the supporting evidence delivered. Stop! The train doors breathe open, and rattle shut. That piece of film could not safely be handed over to the police; in this case, for whatever reason beyond my knowledge, there was no safety in the police, and Chelsea Police Station would be for me (I was convinced) the very valley of death. It is one's wife, child, lover, sibling, parent for whom one carries vengeance to that point of danger. For mere neighbours, folk with whom one has not even broken bread (sherry is not bread, particularly when it has been oxidised to vinegar), for such people one does not follow the vengeance trail wherever it may lead. Nor does the duty of the citizen to uphold the law extend to self-destruction. *Greater love hath no man than this, that he*—but Gavin and his grandmother were not my friends. *It is a far, far better thing that I do now*—not true; it would be a far, far sillier thing; literature has very little application to the problems of real life. And yet I was curious about those photographs. Oh God, I was so curious to know what they would show.

* * *

Both my fear and my curiosity had been increased by an incident earlier in the week. I had returned late on Tuesday evening, after a day of Press Shows, and twelve hundred words of copy written in the office. I always return at the same time on Tuesdays. Perhaps this is known, or perhaps Diana Wapshot, who lives in the flat below, just happened to be glancing through the peep-hole of her front door as I ascended the stairs. For whatever reason, her door opened as I reached the landing, and she confronted me, while upstairs in my own flat, sharp-eared Bonzo gave an anticipatory whine of greeting.

'Still hard at work, Paul?' Whenever and wherever we happened to meet, this was her invariable opening. Either she secretly believed that I did no work, but was kept by my wife, or else she was trying to tell me that, although others would consider the reviewing of films not to be real work, she herself was a person of superior sensibility, well able to recognise the unremitting and lonely toil of the professional writer. Or both. Her husband is a tea-importer in semi-retirement. They have no children, but are visited regularly by a nephew with expectations.

'It never stops,' I said, which was my equally invariable reply.

There was a scratching at my door upstairs. 'You've bought a dog, haven't you?'

'I'm looking after it for a friend.' My lease forbids pets of all sorts, though a blind eye is usually turned to caged birds, cats and miniature dachsunds. I did not believe that Diana would inform on me, but it seemed prudent not to own totally to Bonzo until I had to. No cock crew.

'I couldn't help noticing. It was such a commotion. Henry was lying down. He tries to get a bit of a nap in the afternoons, and that keeps him going for the rest of the day.'

Henry is the husband. I said, 'A commotion?'

'Barking. Growling. Thudding at the door. I had to come out, though I wouldn't interfere normally, as you know. He was so distressed.'

'Henry?'

47

'Your visitor.'

I never have visitors. People come to read the meters, or ring at the downstairs bell to solicit contributions to charity. Carol-singers sing into the entry-phone at Christmas, and there was once a Chinaman, working his way through college by selling magazine subscriptions, who refused to go away. Diana would not describe any such people as these as 'visitors'.

'Did he leave a name?'

'A card.' She produced it. 'He gave me one as well. Such an intelligent man! I suppose you couldn't really call him a visitor—more a canvasser; he was a Social Democrat, doing a survey in depth; he said he was convinced we could be a seed-bed of radical middle-of-the-road political ideas. He had a clipboard, and a checklist, and some pamphlets; I wish our own people were as thorough.' Politically Diana is somewhere to the right of Genghiz Khan. 'He said he was starting at the top of the house, and working down, but when he knocked on your door, all hell broke loose. So I asked him in, and gave him a cup of tea, and we had a right old natter. I told him you're never in on Tuesdays.'

I took the card. There was a name, an address, a telephone number; it was a good address in Cornwall Gardens, where Ivy Compton-Burnett used to live. I said, 'If he was starting at the top, how did he get into the hall?'

'Sorry?'

'If he started at the top, he must have rung my bell first. But I wasn't in to press the entry-buzzer, so how did he get into the hall downstairs?'

'Oh, really, Paul! People always get into the hall.'

'I'd better phone the number on the card. Might as well make sure he exists.'

Doubt was never far below Diana's assured exterior. 'I'll do it.' Upstairs, Bonzo gave an impatient howl. 'That *dog*! We're not supposed to have them, you know. It's a condition of the lease.' She went back into her own hall, and I heard her dialing. I called up to Bonzo to reassure her, but this only provoked the most agitated behaviour; I would have to repaint the door. Diana reappeared, flushed and hostile. 'I've tried twice. Number unobtainable!'

I said, 'He was a burglar, I suppose, one of the gentlemanly ones. It's lucky Bonzo was in the flat; he must have got the shock of his life. It was very brave of you to give him tea.'

'I'll try again through the Exchange,' Diana said, and shut the door in my face.

The man was not, of course, a burglar, of the gentlemanly or any other sort. Flats in the house have been burgled before, the Australians twice, Diana and Henry while they were on an Hellenic Cruise: the first-floor flat is a fortress. A determined burglar would not be greatly hindered by my double locks (he would remove the door from its hinges by applying a jemmy to the frame itself), but such a one would also know my flat to be not worth the effort, since a middle-aged man, living alone and dressed as I dress, is unlikely to own jewellery or precious metals. No, this man, knowing me to be always out until late of a Tuesday, had come with celluloid and picklocks to search the house.

The S.D.P.! Was it a coincidence, or were they trying to tell me something?

They would try again, whoever they were, and they would succeed; they would enter my flat in my absence to search it. And find what? It came to me, after I had already bought the book, that *The Photographer's Handbook* might itself be a cause of danger if it were to be found, since I do not own a camera. I put it away among my books on film, in the small technical section, next to *Notes on the Uses of Mercuric Emulsions in Technicolor Stock*, and hoped it would not be noticed. I have a great many books on film, some of which I have bought for myself, many review copies, and almost the entire technical section acquired free at Trade Fairs, and largely unread.

During the dark hours, and often while I should have been thinking about work, fear and curiosity continued to alternate in my mind, until at last I reached a conclusion.

Thesis: For my own safety, I must destroy the negatives. *Antithesis*: But for my own peace of mind, I must know what has been recorded on them. *Synthesis*: First I must find out what is on them, and then destroy them.

I consulted the *Handbook*, and it seemed to me that my curiosity might be satisfied if I could contrive adequately to follow the process described in the chapter headed 'Making Enlargements Step by Step'. This processs was clearly laid out, with many illustrations but required a Dark Room, fairly elaborately equipped. Perhaps I could adapt a room for what would only be the one occasion (running water was said to be essential), and do without such items as a photographic thermometer, but even so the equipment would cost £208, of which £100 would be the cost of the colour enlarger.

My sources of income are precarious, as has been stated: I should not be able to live where I do if the rent and rates did not allow for mine being an attic flat, or if there were a lift. (I once explored the project of sub-letting the flat during the tourist season in order to augment my income, but was informed disdainfully by one of those estate-agents who deal in such lettings that the rich do not climb stairs.) Nevertheless, I would buy an enlarger if I had to. Perhaps one might be able to find a reconditioned or second-hand model. But where should I hide it, or the rest of the essential equipment?—bottles of chemicals, dishes, clips for hanging the prints up to dry, something called a 'sweep-second timer'. A professional searcher, already looking for a piece of film, would recognise a sweep-second timer and be well acquainted with even reconditioned enlargers.

Clearly I could not entrust the negatives to anyone else to enlarge and print. Equally clearly I could not do the job myself if my flat were to be searched. There was also the danger to Bonzo. These men would not allow her to delay them for long; they would dispose of her ambiguously and without fuss. Poisoned meat? (She was costing me more in meat than I spent on convenience foods for myself.) A street accident? Or simply an information laid to my landlords, some unofficial request from an offical source that I should be instructed to get rid of her? I remembered that I had not yet even bought a dog-licence.

The answer to my immediate problem must be to allow the searchers access to my flat while Bonzo and I were not in it, and the sooner the better. An afternoon walk would not do; they must know about the walks, which, in December weather and with the daylight going early, were of under two hours' duration. They must have decided that they needed longer. They had not found the negatives in Mrs Forbes-Duthie's maisonette, but Gavin might have hidden them anywhere, or even destroyed them; it was unlikely that he would have given them to me, a stranger, but they had to be sure that he had not done so, and it would take time for them to be sure. Very well; they should have time enough. A week-end. The term was over at Hounslow. My next course of evening-classes would begin after the Christmas holiday. I would take Bonzo away from the coming Friday to Sunday, a period during which the whole contents of my flat might be put under a microscope and replaced without my knowledge.

Where? The usual run of hotels, even in winter when they need the custom, are seldom anxious to accommodate alsatians. I consulted a copy of *Our Dogs* at the Reading Room of the Reference Library, and found among the small ads a Guest House in Kendal which welcomed pets. Fell-walking and substantial high-teas were among its other attractions. Bonzo would enjoy walking the fells, and so should I; we would earn our high-teas. Kendal is a long way from London, and I do not own a car, but I remembered that the railways used to sell dog-tickets, and that when I was young, in the days of corridor-trains and separated compartments, dogs often travelled with their owners. There are few corridor-trains nowadays; the carriages of Inter-City expresses have a centre aisle between pairs of seats on either side of a table. Would dogs still be permitted? I telephoned King's Cross, and, after the usual delays, a kindly voice informed me that Bonzo might travel in my company at half price, provided that she did not go about biting the other passengers, in which case she might have to be confined in the van with parcels.

It was so simply and swiftly done—a booking made at the Guest House, tickets for Bonzo and myself from the travel-agent at the corner. I could not, of course, announce my departure in any public way, not even by cancelling the milk and the newspapers since I have neither delivered, but if my telephone were being tapped and any movements moni-tored, the searchers would know. I bought walking-shoes and a camera, and, on consideration, packed *The Photo-grapher's Handbook* with my pyjamas, sponge-bag, a heavy sweater and several pairs of socks. The expense of the trip was inordinate, but most of my purchases were made by credit-card, and would be repaid slowly, month by month, over the coming year.

Such a week-end is, for the purpose of fell-walking, really only Saturday, since much of the Friday and Sunday must be spent in travel. There was a heavy drenching rain. Bonzo and I walked all day in it, eating a packed lunch under the lee of what it was a mockery to call dry-stone walling. Rain obscured the panoramic views. Rain ran down inside the plastic yellow cape, borrowed off Mrs Pendle, whose only guests we were. I slipped twice, bruised my side, and was lucky not to wrench an ankle. It was the greatest happiness. In the evening, I bathed Bonzo in a tin tub in the kitchen, and rubbed her dry, bathed myself and donned scratchy tweeds (borrowed off Mr Pendle) while my own clothes dried, devoured lakes of strong tea, mountains of baps, eggs, bacon, butter, honey, spent the evening by the fire with the Pendles, watching television with Bonzo pressed up against the side of my legs, fell asleep in my armchair, and was guided to bed. No demurral was made at Bonzo's preference for sleeping with me; it seemed to be expected.

* * *

It was charitable of British Rail to allow Bonzo to travel at half-price, for even a docile alsatian takes up the room of three passengers, and one has a table to oneself. On the way back to London, I sat in comfort, reading the Sunday papers, and some way after Preston there came, to destroy my content, the man in the brown suit, walking clumsily down the aisle, carrying two plastic cups of coffee. He put one down in front of me, and sat opposite. Bonzo growled, and I rested my hand on her head.

'Been away for the week-end, then? Very tactful of you. Considerate. We've had a good look round.'

I said, 'I don't know why you're persecuting me like this.'

'Nasty case. Gruesome. Want to get to the bottom of it.'

'But you've been to the bottom of it. He murdered his grandmother, and committed suicide. That was the police announcement.'

'Hatcher, Hatcher, these statements are for the media, not for you and me. Those men weren't policemen. You knew that.' I stared at him. 'There's legitimate police action, and there's illegitimate. Gently jostling some black teenager, high on ganja, that's legit; it is the merest extension of community policing. Lenient kneeling on the kidneys of aggressive drunks—legit again, has to be; you get a nasty class of drunk in the North East. But battering in the heads of old ladies, that's right out of our line. You never thought that was the police?'

'Not at first. Later I couldn't be sure.'

He sighed. 'We're employed to *protect* the public. If only that was better understood! You had a *Photographer's Handbook* in your luggage at the Guest House.'

'If you've been through my suitcase, you'll have noticed that I also have a camera. It's new. I haven't had occasion to take pictures before.'

'You've been reading up on it, have you?'

'The first chapter. It's about how to hold the camera steady.'

'Just checking.' He drained his plastic cup, stood up, and

placed one hand on my shoulder, partly perhaps in a friendly way, and partly because the rocking of the train made it difficult to stand upright without support. 'Get in touch if anyone else contacts you.'

'Such as who?'

'I shouldn't think anyone will. I imagine they got what they came for—found it that night in the old woman's house. We'll keep an eye on you anyway.'

I said, 'If those men weren't the police, why didn't the police interfere on the night of the murder? Where were you?'

'There was no 9 9 9 call, Hatcher. Nobody phoned Chelsea Division. Door broken down, shouts and screams,—' he nodded towards Bonzo—'frantic barking, bloody murder and a spectacular public suicide, but not one of your neighbours phoned the police, because they all thought the police were there already. Neat!' He moved away. He had made no effort to lower his voice during our conversation, and several passengers were staring at him. 'Don't forget to keep in touch.'

One can say anything in public nowadays, and people think it's all done for the television, with hidden cameras.

Nothing was really settled. If the police had guessed that I had spent the week-end away in order to allow them to search the flat without interruption, they would not have expected me to have left anything in it. Of course they had also searched my luggage at the Guest House, but would have assumed that I would keep negatives on my person. I remembered how eager Mr Pendle had been that I should wear his tweeds so as to allow my own clothes to dry properly in the kitchen. Paranoid! One becomes paranoid.

However, if the man in the brown suit had told the truth, there was another interested group besides the police: the four men in uniform had not, in fact, been policemen, but the criminal henchmen of whomever Gavin had been trying to blackmail. The police (*if* I had been told the truth) did not know that these men had not found what they were looking

54

for, did not even know what it was, and the police search of my flat had been no more than a tidying operation of extreme thoroughness. But the four men did know. They knew what they were looking for; they knew they had not found it; they must believe that it had no longer been in Gavin's possession when they had irrupted into the maisonette. They could not know I had it, and Gavin had killed himself before they could force him to tell where it was, but they were bound to consider the possibility. Therefore the man with the scratched face had tried to find out whether I had homosexual tendencies (and might therefore have known Gavin for longer and more intimately than was thought) or political connections.

Why political? Were the pictures in some way political? They were of people, not of documents, not writing or drawings; they were of people whose identities one could not make out, engaged in an activity which could not be identified. However, they had been taken with a miniature camera, which indicated some experience of espionage.

Two points to ponder. The man with a scratched face, although he had not shown her any credentials, had presented himself to my wife as someone engaged on an official enquiry, and had convinced her that this was the case. She had become alarmed on my behalf, she had wondered whether my phone were being tapped, but her fear had been that I might have got myself into trouble in some way with 'the authorities'. Well, he might have been lying, and probably was, but my wife was not easily fooled. Secondly, the man in the brown suit, who, on his own account, should not have known what the four men were searching for (or even, when one considered it, that they were searching for anything at all), had shown a sharp interest in my possession of *The Photographer's Handbook*. It seemed to me that, whether I destroyed the negatives or not, I should continue to be in danger, and whether the man in the brown suit had told the truth or not, I should be imprudent to trust the police.

It seemed to me also that the man in the brown suit must

have been telling the truth in one particular. The police rarely beat to death Senior Citizens of the upper-middle-class in their own homes, if only because it would be hard to prove in court that an arthritic and potentially litigious old lady had actively resisted arrest. The four men could not have been policemen, though there remained a possibility that the police themselves had been instructed to stay away. If I knew for whom the four men were working, that might assist me to evade, or at least in some way placate them, and I might also have a better idea of how far it might be safe to trust the police. To curiosity, therefore, was added self-preservation as a powerful motive for finding out what those negatives depicted.

But I still did not know how to do it.

By the week of Christmas there are few Press Showings, and the cinemas of the West End of London have been given over to 'family entertainment'; films of this kind are often revived from year to year. There were traffic jams, a plastic reindeer in Leicester Square, arches of illuminated snow-geese over Regent Street, and the *Radical*, like the rest of the weeklies, brought out an exceedingly slim issue. I had the Monday afternoon free to walk with Bonzo, and to sit with her afterwards by the electric fire in the sitting-room, growing increasingly sleepy as a defence against what must be done, which was that I must analyse my situation intelligently, and decide upon some positive action.

It is a convenient convention of dramatic fiction (particularly in the field of the television series) that detectives hunt in pairs, so that each piece of simple deduction towards the solving of a case may be explained by one to the other, and so to the audience. How I had despised that convention, believing that in real life the deductive and ratiocinative processes will more usually take place inside one's own head, requiring no confidant, stark mad in white linen like the unhappy lady in *The Critic*! Analysis was my profession. Yet how I longed now for a confidant, for discussion, for a sharing of speculation and response! In real life, it seemed, when it came to any important personal matter, the logical process of deduction ran early into fog.

There was only one person with whom I could discuss my problem in confidence, and know that my confidence would be respected. I telephoned my wife, and invited her out to dinner.

'When?'

'When you like. This evening? Tomorrow?'

'Paul, it's Christmas week.'

Even while we were married, I had resented Christmas as an imposition, and since the divorce had done my best to ignore it. I do not send Christmas cards, and this year had received only three, which remained on my desk. I said, 'I was thinking it might be a Christmas treat. I thought I'd make an effort this year.'

'Alright. Where?'

'We could go to the bistro down the road. Or the Bangkok.'

'God! Do you still go there?'

'I don't go anywhere. I don't like eating in public by myself.' In the days when my wife and I had shared the flat, we had gone often to the bistro down the road or the Bangkok. 'The bistro might be quieter. There's more room between the tables.' If my phone were tapped, as she had speculated and as I now myself believed to be possible, this was as close as I dared go to telling her that I wished to discuss something important. But she would know that already (though tappers, I hoped, would not); why else should I have phoned her at all?

'Right. But not the bistro. I'll pick you up in the car, and take you somewhere nicer.'

'I asked you.'

'You can't afford it, Paul. The B.B.C.'s very stingy about expenses these days, but I'll put you down to research. Can you be ready in an hour? Don't wear anything fancy.'

She hung up before I could protest. She was lying, of

course. It was true that, particularly after the week-end in Kendal and buying the camera, I could not easily afford to take her to dinner even at the bistro, but untrue that she would put me down as expenses. My wife and I, though liberated in so many ways by grammar school and university from the *petit bourgeois* values of our parents, still both had that picky honesty about small amounts of money which is the hallmark of our class.

We dined at Monsieur Thompson, and, on the Monday of Christmas week, almost had the place to ourselves. We could not have been overheard, but my wife nevertheless kept the conversation general, and professed an interest in fell-walking which I cannot believe she truly felt. She refused coffee, saying that we would have it at her flat in Holland Park, where she first insisted on putting on a digital recording of the Pergolesi *Stabat Mater*, a precaution which I considered excessive.

I told her the story so far, and she listened intently with few questions. 'Of course you have to know,' she said. 'Knowing can't bring you into any more danger than you're already in. Have you tried looking at the negatives under a magnifying glass?'

'Without success.'

'You'll have to make enlargements. I suppose you didn't think to bring *The Photographer's Handbook* with you?'

If we'd had the book and the negatives, I think she would have begun that night, and worked on through it. I explained that special equipment was needed, and that I feared to acquire it, in case my flat was searched again.

'Books always tell you to buy more than you really need. A timer! Why can't you just count the seconds? You know—*one* second, *two* seconds, *three* seconds! until you get to sixty; you can check your speed in the light before you have to do it for real. And you don't need special clips to hang the prints up to dry. Stands to reason, any clips will do.' She went to her desk, where groups of papers were clipped together, some by ordinary paper-clips, other thicker groups by spring-clips with handles of bent wire, so that the papers might be easily suspended from some hook or nail. My wife released one such group from its clip. 'Bills!' She brought the clip to me. The bills had been held in two sets of metal lips, enamelled a shiny red with white teeth, and the words 'KISS! KISS!' on the upper lips. 'Present for you! I've always hated it. Now! Trays!'

'Three trays. Developer, stop-bath and fixer.'

'You don't need special trays if it's only to hold liquid. I should think roasting trays would do. You'd have to clean them thoroughly first; I know what you are; you'd get months-old burned fat all over the prints. Or you could use large freezer-trays, the flan-for-a-family-of-five sort; you can get them at the super-market.'

'And the chemicals? Paper?'

'Buy them on the day, so as not to have them hanging about, and throw away the bottles afterwards. You could put them in your briefcase, and flush them down a public loo.'

'I suppose so, if they were small enough. Or a litterbin somewhere in the West End. Enlarger?'

'Ah!' My wife gave herself to thought. The *Stabat Mater* came to the end of Side One, and was turned over. 'Do you remember the days before home movies?'

'There were never any days before home movies. All the early films *were* home movies.'

'There used to be things—Uncle Jack and Auntie May had one. Like a magic lantern. You put in slides of your holiday snaps, and projected them against the wall.'

'Well?'

'What's an enlarger but that?' I had no immediate answer, but it seemed to me that a modern enlarger might incorporate a great many features not to be found on a magic lantern. 'I'll ask someone.'

'No!'

I didn't want her to ask anyone. Let me place that on record now. I had needed to talk to someone, no more than that; I did not wish to involve any other person, certainly not my wife, in my own peril.

I should have known Anne better, did know her better,

and therefore should have known better than to approach her. It was an immediate problem. She was bound to involve herself. 'Well, you can't do it yourself,' she said, 'not if you're being watched. And it's easy for me; I'm always asking people for information; that's my job. And you can't buy the chemicals and the photographic paper either; I'll do that. There was something called "hypo" when I was at school—how it all comes back! A boy called Randall did it; that was his hobby—Gerry Randall. He made me put my hand on the front of his trousers, and we got very friendly for a couple of terms.' My wife had never mentioned the boy Randall to me before. There are things one learns after a divorce which never come up during a marriage, even when it is going sour. 'He had his own Dark Room, the lot—rigged it all up himself. He used to put red tissue paper over the light bulb, and we'd go nearly all the way. *That* had running water. His parents never knew.

'I tell you what,' my wife said, 'did you take any snaps while you were at Kendal?' I had, in fact, used up a whole roll of film, mostly of shots of Bonzo in the rain. It would still be in the camera. 'Send them off to be developed, and ask for slides of the best. That way it'll be natural for you to have a projector, particularly if I buy it for you as a Christmas present.'

Events had begun to move faster than I had anticipated, and it seemed as if I had myself this time begun to take the initiative, or at least my wife had. The end of the *Stabat Mater* was followed on Side Two by a more sprightly piece of orchestral music which must also have been by Pergolesi, or at least attributed to him. My wife said, 'You've suddenly started to interest me again, Paul,' and, reaching up inside my sweater, she undid the buttons of my shirt.

I did not wish to stay the night, knowing that Bonzo would be wondering where I was. Indeed, I suffered a temporary embarrassing detumescence as I imagined her, wandering from room to room, sniffing in corners, searching for me. But after climax was over for both my wife and myself, in that drowsy time of nestling together without speech, I fell asleep, and was woken at six thirty by my wife with a cup of tea.

'I'd have let you sleep on, but it's Tuesday. Have you got a Press Show?'

'Oh God! The Academy. It's something Polish with a buffet lunch. What time is it?'

'Don't worry. You can have a bath here, and I'll run you back.'

We bathed together. She sat between my legs, and I soaped her back. It was like old times, except that we both knew that they *were* old times, and would not return. Dawn comes late in December, and the light was still grey as we drove past the squares, gardens and crescents of the Royal Borough. My wife said, 'I'll find out what I can, and be round on Christmas Eve. Will you be in?' Since it would be a Thursday, I should be in all day, except for the afternoon walk, and even that could be curtailed. She said, 'If we can get everything set up in time, it would be much safer for you to do the enlargements on Christmas Day. These people must take some holidays.'

I pushed open the heavy front door into the communal hall, and saw that the post had already arrived, a clutter of Christmas cards for the other tenants, and one brown envelope addressed to me. On the back of it was a printed instruction that, if it should be undelivered for any reason, it must be returned to Chelsea Police Station. I carried it upstairs. All the pleasure I had been feeling in anticipating the welcome I would receive from that sentimental alsatian waiting for me on the top floor drained out of me, tread by tread, to be replaced by apprehension and fear.

There was welcome, there was reproach, there was a reminder, deposited neatly in a corner of the kitchen by the stack of old newspapers, that we had missed our nightly turn round the square. No damage had been done to furniture or bedding though it was clear that Bonzo had burrowed into the bedclothes and slept between blankets in my absence. I put the brown envelope down on the kitchen table, while Bonzo whined, butted her head into my stomach, held my shoulders with her front paws and licked my face. Did she smell another woman on me? Well, I had bathed, as adulterers do, and cleaned my teeth with Anne's toothbrush. It had not felt like infidelity at the time.

The brown envelope remained. It had to be opened. I opened it. I do not know what I had expected from it, perhaps some curt instruction to present myself for re-examination. Instead there were two strips of photographic negatives inside with enlargements made from them, but no letter. There were more negatives than prints. Some of the snaps I had taken at Kendal were under-exposed, two negatives were entirely black as if the shutter had remained open, and it was clear from many of the prints that I had not fully mastered Chapter One of the *Handbook*, 'Keeping the Camera Steady', but at least four were creditable studies of an alsatian in the rain. I fetched my camera, and opened the back of it. Yes, the film had been removed.

Why had the man in the brown suit bothered to send me the snaps? A joke? A reminder? Harassment to keep me jumpy? A kindly gesture? The last seemed unlikely. The motives of these people were too devious to be deduced.

What interested me more than the snapshots were the negatives enclosed with them, which were each about half an inch square, of the same size as those still contained in the little tube attached to Bonzo's collar. I had imagined some person experienced in espionage, using a miniature camera. It was not necessarily so. The photographs might have been taken with an ordinary Hanimex like my own, the photographer perhaps Gavin himself; he had worked, I remembered, in the Television Department of an advertising agency.

Well, I would know more soon enough.

The matter of the Film Festival was first opened to me on that very Tuesday at the Academy's Buffet Lunch. There was a thin attendance. Many of my colleagues, their deadlines brought forward by Christmas and preferring anyway to spend the week on holiday, must have seen the film at a Magazine Showing some weeks before, or else intended to slip in a review after Christmas, since the Academy Three is a very small cinema, and the film would remain there some time. As for the film itself, it was one of those idyllic, instantly forgettable pieces about small children and farm machinery, set in 1937, with a lot of dappled sunlight and the shadow of the swastika looming near. Such films are commonly made in Eastern Europe, where the shadows of the present time are not considered to be suitable raw material for any form of artistic creation.

The man who approached me was from the trade press—or it may have been an Agency Service; these men look very much alike. He addressed me by my name, and reminded me that we had sat next to each other at the banquet for *Funny Girl*. I had forgotten there ever had been a banquet for *Funny Girl*; it was so long ago. He carried in one hand a full glass of vodka-and-tonic, in the other a plate piled dangerously high with cold cuts, hardboiled eggs, smoked fish and various salads. It is unnecessary to take so much at once, since, if one wishes to make the free meal last all day as I often do, one goes back for further helpings. The man told me his own name—Desmond something—and may have identified himself further, but I was distracted by the beansprouts, grated carrot and lava-flow of mayonnaise which kept slipping off the side of his plate whenever he made any kind of conversational point.

Desmond told me he had always admired my crits, and made a point of reading them in the office every week. The daily papers, he said, and the Sundays too, it was all sensationalism and being clever with them; you got the balanced view from a man like me. He told me that I was not parochial, not like some of these other buggers; I was what he called 'a true man of the cinema' (he repeated that; he was clearly fond of it); I could see beyond my nose to where the artistic action was at. He asked if I ever managed to get away on any of these foreign dos—Cannes, Siena, even Cork; you could get a good glass of champagne, he said, in Cork; you could get the real stuff there; it was a true international forum. He asked me if I would believe that they'd had a great Festival last year at Port au Prince. Manila was the coming place. Had I ever been?

I think I said that the *Radical* was internationalist in principle, but couldn't actually afford to send me abroad, though I usually managed Edinburgh. 'There's ways, Paul,' Desmond said. 'There's ways.' I thought he was about to tap the side of his nose with one finger of the hand holding the plate, but he drew back from it in time, and contented himself with staring at me, sweating, and nodding his head. 'You're not against in principle, then?' he said. 'You'd make a real contribution; I know that. You'll be hearing from me, Paul,' and he moved further down the buffet, and engaged the lady from *Women's Weekly* in what was clearly the same conversation, since I was able to observe, from behind a cascade of cole slaw, her reaction to being classified as a true man of the cinema.

He was a little drunk, I thought, but had asked for nothing as far as I could make out, and certainly I had promised nothing. If later on I were to receive on his account some piece of direct-mail advertising of a quasi-internationalist character, it would go the way of those periodic invitations to apply for an American Express or Diners' Club card, and no harm done. I let the matter fall from my mind, which was already sufficiently occupied with other matters of greater moment.

When my wife arrived, I was scrubbing the grill-pan: the roasting-tin had already been scrubbed. She had said that she knew what I was: the enlargements would be covered in burnt fat. In fact she had forgotten what I was; I am a meticulous washer-up, but was recleaning everything anyway.

She had told me that she would arrive at tea-time, and that the radio should already be playing. A full choir was singing *Unto Us a Child Is Born* as she mounted the stairs. She wore a fur coat and hat, and carried a Harrod's bag full of gift-wrapped parcels. Protruding from the top, and arranged there, I guessed to catch the eye of any watcher, were two Christmas crackers and a small plastic tree.

She unpacked the bag on the kitchen table, and set the crackers and parcels out around the tree, which had a hinged wooden base. Bonzo watched her closely. 'Hullo, dog!' she said. 'You've got a coat just like mine.'

'I'll boil a kettle.'

'Don't bother. I haven't time. Now! Things to tell you! This—' she indicated the largest parcel—'is a slide-projector. It's nothing like as good as a proper enlarger would be, and the light-source is too strong, so you have to cut it down with this' (a small thin parcel) 'which is a six-inch square of smoked glass you have to tape over its light.'

'Oh God!'

'I know. Too complicated for a clumsy gent. But none of it's going to be easy, Paul. Luckily you've got all day for failures.'

I am notoriously maladroit, and have believed this to be due to a lack of sensitivity in the fingers, probably some failure in the function of peripheral nerve-endings. My wife, particularly when we were in the process of falling out, preferred to believe that the lack of sensitivity was congenital, and extended a good deal further than the finger-ends.

I said, 'I've been thinking. Maybe I don't need to make prints at all. If I can just project the negatives themselves onto some blank surface—'

'No good; I've been into that. You get a negative image, with everthing the wrong way round, very difficult to read. And the colours are all strange. Red comes out as green, and yellow is blue, and there's an orange glow over everything; it's just a dog's breakfast.' She glanced at Bonzo. 'Cat's breakfast, if you prefer.' Bonzo's tail moved in what could as easily have been a lash as a wag. 'You'll have to do it by the book, and even then the prints you get won't be up to scratch—black-and-white from colour negs, and rather fuzzy, but can be made out, my informant says.'

'What did you tell him?'

'Nothing. He thinks it's for the programme. A sweet Lancastrian boy with mulberry eyes. Ken. He says we should get to know each other better, but I'm not sure.' She pointed at the parcels. 'Photographic paper, ten by eight. You have to open the packet in the dark, and be careful not to get the paper back to front. Since you're bound to do that, I bought lots. Ken says the emulsion is on the shiny side, if that helps. Chemicals—you dilute them with water; it says how much. Liqueur chocs. A tin of pâté. Harrod's House Claret. Stilton. Now I must rush.'

She kissed me. I said, 'You don't mind if I don't let you know?'

'You're not going to do anything silly?'

'It would be silly letting you know.'

I watched the thoughts click over behind her eyes. My wife was a sort of journalist, after all; it would be torture not to know. I write 'torture', a stupid exaggeration, since I now know what torture is.

'We're not going to stop seeing each other, Paul.'

'No.'

'I'll let time pass, and then get it out of you.' She kissed me again, more warmly. 'Bye, love. Bye, Bonzo.' I boiled the kettle anyway, and Bonzo and I had a cup of tea.

My wife always went to Torquay at Christmas to see her parents; I used to go with her. My own parents are dead, so Christmas Day was, for me, a day like any other, except that there were fewer distractions. No watcher (if there were watchers) would expect me to leave the house except to exercise Bonzo, so it was a particularly suitable day for what I had set myself to do.

There were two possible choices for a Dark Room, the kitchen and the bathroom, since both had running water. The kitchen would have been more convenient, because the table would have provided a stable surface for the trays of chemicals, but I chose the bathroom. The kitchen window was not curtained. I had sellotaped newspapers together to make a light-excluding screen, and this might be noticed from any of the houses opposite when placed over the kitchen window, whereas the bathroom curtains are usually closed anyway, and the screen might be tacked in place behind them.

The other curtains which were usually drawn, at least at night, were those of the bedroom, in which there were two light wooden bookcases against one wall. I had already removed the books from one, and, before opening the bedroom curtains, I took it to the bathroom, and placed it, shelf side down, over the bath, so that its back made a sort of table.

I used the roasting-tin for developer, the grill-tray for fixer, and the small washing-up bowl (also thoroughly cleaned) as a stop-bath; with containers so different, it would be hard to get them confused in the dark. Two clothes-pegs as tongs. *The Photographer's Handbook*, from which I must work, assumed the use of an enlarger; all its instructions, written and pictorial, were for that, and would have to be adapted to allow for a slide-projector as I went along. I had made a cardboard mount for the strip of film, and had cleaned the negatives as well as I could with a soft paintbrush. The mount could be moved as if it were a slide, projecting each negative in turn. The photographic paper was supposed to be placed on a kind of easel under metal masking strips, and the position of this easel was shown as being horizontally below the enlarger-head. A slide-projector, however, unless one can command an astonishing steadiness of hand, functions vertically. My easel would have to be vertical, and I assumed that the size of the picture would be controlled by the distance of the easel from the projector.

My easel was of stiff white card, much larger than the picture size, kept from tilting backwards or falling forwards by books behind and books on either side in front. Over it was placed, instead of metal masking-tapes, a piece of black card, in which a square of the desired picture-size had been cut, and the projector was manoeuvred until its enlargement of the negative exactly fitted this space. My wife's informant, Ken, had spoken the truth. The projection of the first negative showed me only that five human figures were depicted, three standing, one lying, and one in a position which was more like crouching. I assumed that the activity was in some way sexual: one makes such an assumption when blackmail is in the case. The projections of the later pictures were similar, though the positions of some of the participants changed, and the colours were, as I had been warned, distinctly odd, with a great deal of green.

I had set up the equipment with the bathroom light on, switched to the light of the projector only, as I manoeuvred the projected image into the space designed for it, and must next, in total darkness, take a piece of photo-sensitive paper from the packet, close the packet carefully, and then place the paper, emulsion side outwards, between my two pieces of card. I had anticipated difficulty; I had not anticipated terror. The bathroom door was closed, the newspaper screen efficiently in place. I switched off the light of the projector and was engulfed in blackness. There was a floor, because I was standing on it, but no walls or ceiling. Yet there was no sense of space either; the blackness pressed in on me, closer than walls, hugging me, imprisoning me. It was my coffin, and the earth around the coffin, and black night all about the earth in which I had been buried alive. I dropped the unopened packet of printing-paper, and it was gone, fallen away into the blackness. I must not move; I would knock over the slide-projector, and break it; I would upset the chemicals. I moved. A sharp edge, which must have been the bookcase, struck out at me, wounded my knee, and retreated again into the blackness. It should have been possible to feel my way along the side of the bath towards the door and so to the light-switch. Instead my body became rigid, my knees bent, my trunk leaning forwards, halfway to the foetal position, my arms hugging my shoulders. The blackness controlled me, and would not allow me to look for light.

The state would have passed. The blind must live in such

blackness all their lives; I myself spend much of my professional life in what is at least gloom. But it did not seem to me then that the state would pass, and if it did, I should have gone mad first. I was saved by two circumstances. I had begun to moan or whimper, I suppose, to make some kind of noise induced by fear, or perhaps my fear itself could be sensed, and it was answered from outside by Bonzo, who began to whimper in reply, and scratch at the door. This gave me a knowledge of direction, as well as companionship, and as I stretched out my right arm to where the door must be, I saw light. The dial of my wristwatch was radiant, and glowed on my wrist, returning sight to me and a sense of the passage of time. The darkness receded a little, the fear much more. I reached the door, opened it to daylight, and consoled my dog.

Mulberry-eyed Ken might decently have warned my wife of the claustrophobic effect of total darkness. Well, I had experienced it now, and would be able to bear it, since only the placing of the paper demanded such a condition. The experience had also been helpful in reminding me that my watch had a second hand. I would not have to count aloud. I should be able to time the various processes, even in darkness.

Everything was improvised. There were failures; I had four attempts at the first print before I could make anything of it at all. Even success was fuzzy. My assumption was proved correct; the activity was sexual. Four of the figures were men of middle age; the fifth—recumbent—seemed to be a boy of about sixteen. I had decided that, since even my first successful print lacked definition, I would develp all six, and examine them in detail when they were dry. But as each picture appeared beneath the surface of the developing liquid in the roasting-pan, one could see generally what was going on. The first picture aroused distaste in me, the third anger. At first a light grey, then darker, clearer, the elements separating into degrees of darkness, it was like looking into a magic pool, but what was shown was not pleasing. With the fourth picture, I began to sweat, with the fifth to shake;

at the sixth, I vomited into the bowl of the W.C. and knelt by it, retching. The sixth print was, in consequence, over-developed, but I did not make another. They would all have to be destroyed, in any case.

All the colours are strange: the red comes out as green. The projected image of the sixth negative had green all over.

I knelt by the bowl of the W.C. There was a taste of bile in my mouth, and cold in my bones. The tears in my eyes were only partly due to vomiting. I could hear Bonzo outside the door; again she had picked up my distress. I wished very much that I had never found the strip of film in her collar. I wished that I had burned it when I found it. I wished that I had not made the prints.

The door-buzzer sounded. I thought, 'They have come for me. I don't care.' It was only carol-singers, a sponsored group in aid of Cancer Research. I had nothing smaller than a five-pound note, and took it down to them. Diana was in the hall, and the Australians. We wished each other a Merry Christmas, and I declined the offer of wassail.

I returned to the bathroom. I emptied the chemicals into the sink, ran the tap a long while, took the three containers back to the kitchen, and washed them. I returned the bookcase to the bedroom, and replaced the books. The six prints were hanging by clips to a string over the bath; I averted my gaze from them. I removed the taped newspapers from the bathroom window. There was underwear soaking in the kitchen sink. I rinsed it, placed a clothes-horse on the taped newspapers, and draped the underwear over it to dry. The washing-up bowl was no longer a stop-bath; I filled it with dirty drying-up cloths, and added warm water, detergent and bleach. A frozen chicken, stuck with garlic and rubbed with dried tarragon, was placed in the roasting-pan: it was Christmas Dinner. The grill-pan was used to make toast, which I ate with a mug of tea and an aspirin at the kitchen table. I put the slide-projector back in its box, and left it among a litter of coloured wrapping-paper with the two crackers and the other presents of liqueur chocolates, pâté, claret and cheese, next to the plastic Christmas tree. In a copper bowl, in which usually a plant stood, I burned the rest of the photographic paper, and flushed the ashes down the W.C. The prints would follow soon enough, and I would wash out the bath, and then bathe in it. The smoked glass and bottles which had contained chemicals would be taken out with Bonzo and myself for our walk, and I would try to lose them in Earl's Court.

I was reasonably sure, and would be completely so when I had examined the prints in detail, that I knew one of the four middle-aged men.

RICH AND STRANGE

IT IS NOT SURPRISING THAT I KNEW THE MAN. ONE OF THE consequences of an Oxbridge education is that, by the time one reaches one's late forties, many of one's contemporaries have become public figures. I have appeared, bare-kneed, in a play by Christopher Fry at a Y.W.C.A. just off St Ebbe's with someone who later became Minister for Education, have fielded at short-leg to the bowling of an incipient bishop (I still have the scar), and am on nodding terms with the Chairman of British Rail. Of the staff of the undergraduate magazine, *The Isis,* during the time I was its film critic, only one member besides myself has pursued a career in journalism, and has spent the last twenty years as a political columnist in making a graceful public progress rightwards from just left of centre, but one of the others is a well-known poet, now resident in California, another the headmaster of a minor public school; the gossip columnist runs his own Public Relations firm. Undergraduates with whom I had some small social contact are now to be found among the higher echelons of the Civil Service, the B.B.C., the British Council and the Arts Council; others manage commercial television companies or advertising agencies; several are Members of Parliament, of whom a few go in and out of Cabinet, and some hang about at its fringes as Junior Ministers and Parliamentary Private Secretaries. Some have made reputations as actors, composers, novelists, academics (or, more commonly, novelists who are also academics); others may direct films in Hollywood or operas at Glyndebourne, head publishing houses or hold professorships of Military History. In the law courts, on the boards of multi-national companies, in the universities, the hospitals—look for them; they are there. Only the Trades Unions have escaped their influence. So it is not surprising that I knew one of the men. You may think I should have known all four.

The man I knew, the man who with his fellows had made the progress, recorded in those six paragraphs, from buggery to butchery, who had taken part communally first in the sexual assault, then the humiliation, the torture and finally the murder of a bound and terrified teenage boy, had bathed in his blood, smeared it over himself and his fellows, licked it from his hands—I must write this, the full enormity of it, though even now, remembering, my stomach turns over—that man, since he was a Minister of Her Majesty's Government, might have been recognised by many, but I had known him personally, had known him as an undergraduate; he had been my contemporary. I had not known him well. His interests were mainly political, while my own energies were dissipated in various other directions— literary, theatrical, the Film Society and, in an enthusiastic but unskilful way, sport. There were, and probably still are, so many college and university societies, a maze of delightful avenues all leading away from work, but it was said of him that he would only join those of which he could make himself president. Our paths would not have crossed, except that we shared a tutorial for a term, and every fortnight his tutor and I would be treated to his accomplished reading of essays which reduced the philosophies of Aristotle, Hobbes, Bentham, Marx and Proudhon to the intellectual level of *The Reader's Digest*—it was an alpha performance of gamma material; he was bound to become a professional politician.

And then, fifteen years later, at a college Gaudy, late at night, both of us drunk and pissing on hollyhocks in the Fellows' Garden, he had wept on my shoulder, and cried, 'I have wasted my life, Paul. Paul . . . Wotsit . . . I have wasted my life.'

It was necessary to clear my thoughts. A reviewer makes notes, writes drafts, knows what he means as he sees what he says. I could put nothing on paper, so I made notes in my head.

First, the identities of those whom I thought of as 'the watchers', who were searching for the negatives and had hunted Gavin and killed his grandmother. My wife had believed that the man with the scratched face had been some kind of official agent, presumably someone for MI 4, 5 or 6; they are like motorways, these secret departments of state. Well, that might be so; it could not be ruled out. Certainly a Minister of the Crown might command the services of such agencies, but only in his public capacity, never for private reasons, not as a defence against blackmail for murder. The first act of any such agency would be to remove the Minister, as a security risk, before hunting down the blackmailer. Since the Minister still occupied his position, attended Cabinet, and was, one must assume, privy to state secrets, the only way in which a government agency could be involved would be if it suspected that the Minister was a security risk, and was looking for evidence to prove it, in which case they would be working against the Minister, not under his orders. If that were the case, my best course would be to give up the negatives, but I did not believe that this was the case. We are told that such people are, like James Bond, licensed to kill in the course of their duties, but I did not believe that they had killed the old lady.

If the four bogus policemen were acting for the Minister, it was unlikely that they were from the secret services, my wife's conviction and the curious behaviour of the Chelsea Police notwithstanding. But one had to consider also that they need not be his agents at all; there had been partners in the crime, any one or all of whom might have such agents in their employment.

A teenage boy, bound, abused, and murdered—to do that, perhaps not for the first time, perhaps to other boys, and keep it secret, would require great power and much money. The Minister had influence, but little real power, and although he was no doubt comfortably off, with his ministerial salary and some income from shares, was not rich as the rich are rich. I closed my eyes, and tried to see through his, tried to be him for a while. Perhaps at first it had been only a small taste, seldom exercised, for boys and for hurting boys. *'I'm not hurting you, am I? Do say if I am.'* Perhaps, at school, at university, even later, it had been a matter of mock-wrestling, playing at punishment, perhaps if and when it came to bought sex, as it would if he were married and the taste had to be secretly indulged, the recipient would pretend more pain than was felt, and all parties would be satisfied. (I did not go to public school myself, but the Minister would have done so. Were prefects still allowed to beat younger boys in his day?) So it would have been at first, and later, perhaps on a visit to New York or Amsterdam . . . well, I had no experience of such matters, and found that my imagination would not carry me so far. But I imagined that someone who knew of such a taste in the Minister, and shared it, might find it easy enough to arrange an encounter, easy to inflame the imagination with hints of what was possible, easy to initiate him into ways of inflicting pain both more sophisticated and more direct, his conscience perhaps bemused by drugs and by the knowledge that it was all paid for and didn't matter, until at last he was drawn into an excess of behaviour of which he would not have believed himself capable, did not anticipate or intend when he started, went step by step with others, encouraged by the actions of others, and now (I imagined him now), now that it was done, lay awake as I did, sweating and shuddering at the memory. *'Paul . . . Wotsit . . . I have wasted my life.'*

I have the liberal imagination, you see. I find excuses.

If it were like that, at all like that, then the man with money and power, the man who could organise the affair and keep it secret, might enjoy not only the act itself, but as a secondary benefit might enjoy the corruption of well-known people; he might enjoy that for its own sake, and also for the use he could make of it. If that were so, then at least two of the other men in the picture might be well-known, public faces. I must try to find out. If that were so, then the four bogus policemen might be the agents of such a man, and I was in great danger. The thought was almost overwhelming, *'Get out of this while you can. Go to the police, the man in the brown suit, anyone with the power to protect you.'* But I continued to distrust the police. Again I reminded myself that any watchers could not know that I had the negatives, that Gavin might have hidden them, destroyed them, or given them to someone else; indeed he never had given them to me, a comparative stranger, and I had only found them by accident. The probability was that I did *not* have the negatives, and as long as I did nothing to arouse suspicion, the watchers would continue to look elsewhere, and in time forget me. I reminded myself of that.

I turned my imagination to Gavin. I must see through his eyes also, eyes of the deepest blue with dark lashes, into which I had once gazed, and felt a wivvery feeling. Events go wrong; that was the key. I did not believe that he had been party to a planned murder, yet he must have been concerned somehow, must have been present, concealed, and taken the photographs, or else had received them from whomever had taken them. *Events go wrong.* He was capable of blackmail, because he had tried it. Suppose that he had never known what was intended, but had been in some way a party to the procurement of the boy, had supposed that he could take photographs of what he assumed would be no more than an orgy with trimmings and use them for his own purposes, that he had been shocked, terrified by what had occurred, but had taken the pictures anyway. I found that I could believe that, and could believe also that Gavin might persuade himself that blackmail was, therefore, a punishment, the well-deserved punishment of an atrocious act.

What followed? What was hidden in Bonzo's collar was a roll of six negatives, not unexposed film. The presumption must be that Gavin had himself developed the film, and perhaps made prints, which he would have sent to his intended client, or clients—to the public faces, not the man with money and power. There would have been difficulties. It is hard to deal privately with public people. Secretaries open their letters, sometimes even those marked 'Personal'. Any missive sent by post would have to bear some sort of identification of origin on its outside. Six contact prints in an envelope would not look much like a bomb; nevertheless, politicians these days are increasingly reluctant to open anonymous mail. Would the delivery have to be in person? What a risk!—unless Gavin or someone with whom he collaborated already had access.

I must consider also the actual process by which the film had been developed. Gavin, the papers had stated, had worked in the Art Department of an advertising agency, so it was likely that he would be experienced in photography. Would the agency have a Dark Room of its own which he might have used after office hours? My impression was that advertising agencies do not usually bother with such matters, preferring to hire professionals. Certainly Gavin would know professional photographers. Again there was the possibility of a collaborator. He had not mentioned one to me, but he had said so little of the whole affair to me.

Of course, if I could deduce so much, the watchers must have done so too.

Was the boy a lead? Had television and the newspapers been carrying pictures of a sixteen-year-old boy, missing from his home? If I spent a morning looking through back copies of the popular papers, would I find the face? No. With unemployment over three million, boys of that age left home every day, with very little notice taken of their going. I could not even be sure that the boy was British, or that his murder had taken place in Britain, since the fuzzy background was only of a room, with no clues to its geography.

Was it 'only a room?' Was it not more like a Turkish Bath or sauna? Had the boy not been lying on a slab of some sort?

There was no doubt in my mind that something must be done; the boy's blood cried out for vengeance. I have been opposed to capital punishment all my thinking life, but I would have brought back the rack, the block, the gruesome disembowelling of the Tudors to punish whoever had been responsible for that mutilation and murder.

It seemed to me that there were two steps to be taken as soon as could be. I must find out the identities of the three men with the Minister; if my supposition were correct, at least two should be public figures. I must also try to find out who was Gavin's collaborator, if he had one. And I must follow these lines of enquiry without doing anything to arouse the suspicions of the watchers, in case they were still watching, since any action of such a sort on my part would tell them at once that I knew of the existence of the negatives, even if I did not have them. I must follow my usual daily routines exactly; any action performed outside the framework of those routines must have an obvious and innocent explanation.

Do I appear resolute? I was not resolute. I have summarised a process of thought which occupied my mind for four days and three nights, a period of indecision, lethargy and fear between Christmas and the end of the old year. On the fourth day, December 29th, my wife telephoned.

'Aren't you going to say thank-you for your presents?'

'I've been meaning to phone you, but I wasn't sure when you'd be back.'

'I'm back. Phone me. Did you have a fun Christmas? Nor did I. The latest thing with my dad is circulation problems; they've quite taken over from going to Sales. He has to lie on his shoulders, with his legs up the bedroom wall, for half an hour a day. I got to hold his legs still; that was the high point of my holiday. I suppose you and Bonzo had great romps.'

'Should I take you out somewhere?'

'What an old-fashioned gentleman you are, love! You don't have to take ladies out nowadays before you go to bed with them, particularly your ex-wife. I'll pick you up at seven.'

I said to my wife in the car, 'I dare not tell you. The knowledge is too dangerous.'

My wife said, 'Ah!'

It threw something of a blight over the evening, but I knew I had done the right thing.

The first part of my task would not be as difficult as the second. I should, in prudence, have burned all six of the fuzzy enlargements; in fact, I had kept the first for reference, though I could think of nowhere safer to keep it than with the credit cards in my wallet. I hoped I should not need to do so for long. The *Radical* has nothing like the facilities of a national, or even a regional newspaper, but there is what is called 'the Library'; it consists of two shelves of reference books. Any newly-published work of reference which is not actually given out for review (and very few are) finds its way onto these shelves. In addition, there are back numbers of *Stern, Paris-Match* and *The Illustrated London News* kept in piles in a corner. I should be able to make time, when I was alone in the office after writing my copy on a Tuesday, to consult the books and look through the pictures in the magazines. I must not make too much time, of course; the watchers would know what time I usually returned on a Tuesday.

In the event, I was lucky. I began my search on the first Tuesday of the new year, which was January 4th, worked through the previous year's issues of *The Illustrated London News,* found the Minister's face roughly once a fortnight, but none of the others. On the Friday, making my usual visit to pick up that week's copy and display my availability for further work, I saw among the pile of books for review a large, expensively produced volume entitled *Famous Faces, a Pictorial Who's Who of the World Today.*

'May I take that?'

'You want to sell it, I suppose? Let me see.' My editor looked at the price. 'Nineteen, ninety-five! That's office perks, Paul.'

'I'll bring it back.'

'Oh, sell it if you like. Who cares? We'll all be on the streets soon enough.' The *Radical* had made a small annual loss for the last two years. This is a fact over which the editor brooded constantly, and I chose not to brood at all; if unemployment came, it came, and must be faced when it came. I took the book, which I returned the next week, having found two of the other faces.

Both were Americans. The first was a N.A.T.O. general, a graduate of West Point, married with two teenage children, a career soldier; he was unlikely to be the man with power and money. Over the second, I was in more doubt. He was an aide to the President. I am not sure what the function of an aide is within the governmental structure of the U.S.A.; in spite of the feminine ending, they do not often seem to be women. This was a 'special aide'. Perhaps he had not been special enough. I remembered, now that I saw the face, that he had been in trouble; there had been allegations of corruption, something to do with his having known that silos for nuclear missiles were to be built in Arizona, and his first wife's brother was discovered to have bought the land. There was no direct connection which could be proved, since ex-wives are no longer one flesh, and the President had stood by his aide. Nevertheless there had been a stink in the air. It was odd that the editors of *The Illustrated London News* should have missed him, but their policy is, pictorially speaking, to accentuate the positive.

Three public faces, then—a Minister, a general, and an aide—of whom one, if the allegations of corruption were true, might also be rich and powerful.

It was the third week of January. I had made progress, but I had done nothing. I began to understand how a paranoid schizophrenic must feel. I had told myself not to vary any of my usual routines, and one would think that to be easy enough. It is not. I had to behave as though I were under constant surveillance, and also as if I were not being watched at all, to be forever wary, yet seem innocent and ordinary. *Had it been safe to have brought that book home? Had it been noticed as I carried it in the street, sat with it in* the underground? My hearing grew sharper, but also misleading, because I could not be sure whether I heard what I had heard, or had imagined it. I picked up fragments of conversation from people on an Up escalator as I passed on a Down, and attempted to give them significance. Of all the various clicks, crackles and buzzes with which British Telecom afflicts our telephones, I tried to pick out those which might indicate a tap. Among the faces of other passengers on bus or tube whom I saw on my way to or from work, I tried to recognise any which might have become familiar through being often near me. I dared not vary in any significant way the times or places of my walks with Bonzo, but I tried to vary my approaches to Kensington Gardens, and became uneasy if it seemed as though a fellow walker, even a fellow dog-walker, were accompanying me for too long in the same direction.

I continued to spend one evening a week with my wife, since that pattern had been established, and usually stayed the night, to Bonzo's grief. At the end of the month, my wife, having waited as long as she considered reasonable, examined the contents of my wallet one morning while I was still asleep, and found the fuzzy enlargement. 'I don't call that so awful,' she said, as she brought me tea. 'Not these days. He'd have to resign, of course. Still, it doesn't explain killing the old lady.'

I knew at once what had happened. I said, 'That's only the first picture. It doesn't stop at that.'

My wife said, 'Ah!'

'It ends in murder. They murder the boy while he's still tied up. I don't want to talk about it.'

'Who are the others?'

I told her as much as I had discovered.

'Are you sure you're wise to keep the picture?'

'There's one man I still can't identify.'

'And what will you do when you can?'

To my surprise, I began to weep. My wife held me. I pushed my head between her breasts, and moved my face from side to side, while she kissed my hair. I found this comforting.

I said, 'My work's been suffering. I'm making no progress with Clint Eastwood at all. Sometimes I can sit all the way through a Press Show, and find I can't remember anything about the film; I have to consult the synopsis before I write my review.'

'I could help you.'

'No. Please, no! Promise me you won't ask any questions. Talk to nobody. They don't care about killing people.'

'Promise me that when you know what you're going to do, you'll discuss it with me first.' I promised, but I did not intend to keep my promise.

Time had passed, an insupportable situation going monotonously on; as in real life it often does; it is not like the movies. Film is all exterior, all action, cause leading at once to effect, and the inter-acting effects tumbling over each other to a conclusion; there is even a device of film-narrative called 'simultaneous action', as if one line of action were not enough. But in real life, at least in my own life, it had been all interior, a terrified indecision, in which days had passed, and now weeks, with, as it seemed to me, no action at all.

I had to become agent again, not patient. There was still the question of Gavin's collaborator, if he had one, to be explored. I must first, therefore, devise an innocent reason for my enquiries, and make sure that it was known. Once again, Bonzo must come to my aid. She had been a great joy to me during all this time. I had drawn strength from her, and found that her being with me helped me to sleep.

I presented myself at Chelsea Police Station, and asked to see the inspector. He did not keep me waiting, but came bustling into the Interview Room with his documents and pad of A4 lined paper.

'I'm rather embarrassed. It seems such a small thing.'

The inspector gave me what must have passed, amongst the Chelsea Police, for an encouraging smile. 'Nothing is too small in a case of this nature, Mr Hatcher. You must allow us to judge.'

'It's about the dog.' His smile faded. 'I think she ought to be mated. I've had her some time. She'll be coming into season soon.'

'You've requested an interview, because you wish to mate your dog?'

'I'd need the pedigree.'

'Yes?'

'I couldn't get a stud for her without it. I was thinking . . . Well, you must have searched the young man's flat. Examined his effects. It must have been there.'

'The pedigree of Mr Durston's dog would not be the focus of any such investigation.'

'No, I see that. But if you'd kept the papers . . . still had them in a file somewhere.' It required some courage to continue with this masquerade. 'Tucked away.'

'It would not *be* tucked away. It would have been destroyed.' He put the top back on his fountain pen, and stood up. Events were repeating themselves. 'I'm sorry we can't help you.'

'If you knew any of his friends.'

'What?'

'If I could know the names of his friends, and how to reach them, one of them might know the breeder.' I explained. 'Wherever he'd bought Bonzo, the breeder would have a copy of the pedigree. It would be very helpful if I could find the breeder. I could ask advice about a suitable mate.'

'We're always anxious to assist the public, but this goes beyond our terms of reference, Mr Hatcher.'

'I'm sorry. I've wasted your time.'

'That is one way of putting it.'

'There was a friend mentioned in the papers after the incident. An antique-dealer, someone like that. I could look up back numbers in the Reference Library, and try to find him. I'll do that. I'm so sorry to have bothered you.'

I let myself out of the Interview Room. The inspector remained where he was, looking after me.

In the evening, the man in the brown suit came calling. "You want to mate that bitch of yours, I hear?'

'I thought it would be a fulfilment for her.'

'Messy business. Could turn her savage.' He looked round the living-room. Bonzo was couched at my side. 'You've no room for pups.'

'I thought of selling them. There's a market for pedigree alsatians. You know I don't make much money.'

'Wreck the furniture.'

There seemed to be a whistle in the room, which had not been noticeable before his arrival. I wondered if he were wearing a pace-maker, or had trouble with his false teeth. My wife's mother has had a series of hearing-aids, all of which made such a noise, but a plain-clothes policeman could hardly be expected to function if he were deaf. It might have been anything. People these days seem to have mechanical aids for so many conditions. The building-supervisor of the flats, Mr Mathieson, on a visit to see about the guttering, had once taken off his shirt to show me a colostomy-bag. He was not allowed to eat spinich, or any abrasive foods.

'I thought I'd try to find one of Mr Durston's friends, and ask. There was someone quoted in the papers—Damian someone—an antique-dealer.'

'Interior decorator.'

'I thought he might know where—'

'Dead.'

One could hear the whistling noise quite clearly in the silence. I was allowed to be shocked. I was not allowed to suspect foul play, except that the coincidence was clearly striking.

I said, 'It seems an odd coincidence.'

'Nothing odd about it. Picked up a piece of rough in a pub off King's Cross. Beaten up and robbed. Died of it. Happens. They lead a chancy life, these queers: I'm an old-fashioned sort of a man, I can't say 'gays', can't bring myself—too far from the truth. You've no inclinations in that line, I suppose?'

'I think you know I haven't.'

'Why should I?'

'There was a man making enquiries. My wife told me—positive vetting, she thought. It was just before Christmas.'

'Nothing to do with me. Go to bed with what you like, as long as it's over twenty-one.'

'Did they find the murderer?'

'Not my case.' A small card appeared as if from his sleeve. 'I got the breeder's name. Wrote it down for you. Mrs Emily Stevenson. Warmington. It's a small village near Banbury. You'd better get in quick; they're going to run a motorway through it.'

'You're very kind.' I was no nearer any of Gavin's friends, but had acquired the obligation to get Bonzo mated, and to rear and sell the pups. I said, 'There's a funny whistling noise in here. I think it may come from you.'

'Oh, that! . . . Well, you've got a bug, haven't you?' It was possible that the man in the brown suit had received training as a conjurer. Perhaps he still performed at children's parties. What he now produced was something which looked like a miniaturised transistor radio. The whistling sound was coming from that. 'Always carry this little fellow when I'm making a professional call.'

'But that's ridiculous. Why should anyone bug me? What could they hope to hear? Nobody ever comes here, except occasionally my wife. I never talk to anyone but Bonzo.'

'Routine procedure. I don't expect they're still bothering to listen. Should have been collected, but people don't take the trouble. We're a disposable society, that's what it is.'

' "They"?'

'Could be us. I can't remember. If it was just routine, I'm not to know. Could be anybody. I'll get rid of it.' He took something which I did not see from behind a lithograph of a wild dog by Elizabeth Frink, given to me by my wife, and dropped it into his pocket. The whistling noise stopped.

'You seem to know exactly where to find it.'

He tapped the little radio-thing. 'Magic.'

'May I have the bug?'

'I'll keep it for you.' He held out a hand to Bonzo. 'Shake a paw?' Bonzo looked at me, and, feeling a fool, I nodded. The man took Bonzo's paw, and shook it gravely. She endured it. 'Tell you what,' he said. 'If it's just her emotional fulfilment you're after, it doesn't matter what dog gets one up her. You just wait until she comes on heat, and take her for one of your little walks in the Park. You'll be surprised at the attention.'

I opened the door for him. 'I told you, I want to sell the puppies.'

Of course it could not have been a coincidence. Had this Damian man been Gavin's collaborator? Is that why he had been killed? 'Beaten up, and died of it'—they would have been beating information out of him; it was the treatment Gavin had jumped from the roof to avoid. Did that mean that the watchers now knew that Damian did not have the negatives? Would that bring them closer to me? Considered in this light, the episode of the bug might have done me good if anyone had been listening; it had shown me as the innocent and foolish person I wished to seem to be, and perhaps for most of the time was.

I reminded myself that I had only the word of the man in the brown suit that there had actually been a bug behind the picture. I had not been allowed to see the object itself.

Slowly, reluctantly, over several days, I came to decide on a third line of action, which was not to enquire, but to expose, and get the whole business over. I must make enlarged prints of the negatives, many copies of each, and send them out broadcast to newspapers, radio and television. This could not be done in the flat with improvised equipment, because it would take too long, with the consequent risk of discovery, and because of the poor quality of the prints. Fuzzy prints of the kind which I, at the rate of one to each negative, had taken most of Christmas

Day to achieve, would not reproduce in newsprint or on television, and could easily look like fakes. They would provoke enquiry, cause embarrassment, but might allow the main protagonists time to evade exposure and punishment. They would also almost certainly lead the watchers back to me, whereas enlargements of a professional standard would lead away.

I dared not enlist a helper (certainly not my wife and her mulberry-eyed Ken), but I must procure access to professional equipment, and in such a way as not to alert the watchers. How? I would take a leaf out of Gavin's book, and explore the potentialities of my place of employment, or at least my part-time employment, the East Hounslow College of Further Education, where evening classes in Photography were popular and well-attended. Somehow I would avail myself of the College facilities. I would wear rubber gloves to make the enlargements, gloves of soft leather to buy envelopes of the most common sort from a self-service supermarket, and would not lick the stamps, lest I should be identified by my saliva. I would address the envelopes (still wearing gloves) by ball-point pen in block capitals, sloping backwards from the usual direction of my own handwriting. The pen would be destroyed after use, and I should post the envelopes at the Trafalgar Square Post Office at a particularly busy time.

How much, I wondered, would it cost to make a very short film, to be written by my own pupils, and produced in conjunction with those of the Photographic Course? Too much—the cost of stock and of processing would be more than the College could afford, and anyway, if we were to use film stock, the Dark Room at the College might not be able to cope. No. I had it! My pupils would write the film, and those of the Photographic Course would produce a series of stills, from which we should co-operatively construct a detailed storyboard. I should be able to make full use of the photographic facilities of the College, without arousing any suspicion. It would take time to set up, but it could be done.

Another thought fell like a shadow across my self-congratulation. Was it possible that the negatives themselves had been faked? There is so much one can do technically. One could certainly transfer four men from one background to another, and simulate blood and wounds. But one could not strip the men. Even if one had found all four together in a Turkish Bath without towels and photographed them without their knowledge, even if one could graft erections onto flaccid members, their actions could not have been simulated. Lookalikes?—four lookalikes? Or, if grafting were in question, to graft public faces onto naked private bodies? It would not do. The reaction to Gavin's attempted blackmail had been too violent. The four bogus policemen had not been searching for cleverly contrived fakes.

Meanwhile it seemed safer to burn the last of the fuzzy enlargements, which I had been keeping in my wallet. I should not forget the faces of the general and the aide, and as for the fourth man, under my new plan the media would identify him. I broached the project of a co-operatively produced storyboard to my class, who received it enthusiastically. I left a note in the pigeon-hole of the Head of the Department of Graphic Art and Design. On the morning after doing so, the Saturday of the third week of February, I received through the post an invitation to be a member of the International Jury of a Film Festival to be held in the Principality of Liechtenstein. All my expenses would be paid, and there would be an honorarium of five thousand Swiss francs. I was asked to signify my acceptance to the Festival Director in Vaduz as soon as possible, since arrangements for the Festival, to be held in the last week of March, were already well advanced. The Festival Director took it upon himself to be assured that his distinguished colleague (myself: I was addressed as 'Distinguished Colleague' throughout) would wish to be associated with such an international cultural occasion of the first magnitude, since not only had there never been a Film Festival in the Principality before, but also the Festival itself was the first to take as its theme the most advanced developmental aesthetic in cinematography today.

The letter of invitation was in English of a sort, inasmuch as, even if I could not be sure what an advanced developmental aesthetic was, one could get the general drift. The brochure which accompanied it, and which no doubt explained the theme of the Festival in more detail, was in German, a language which I neither speak nor understand. But it was well printed and laid out on glossy paper, and illustrated with what I assumed to be stills of films not yet released in Britain. There was also a map of Liechtenstein, showing the location of all the Public Swimming Baths, and a photograph of the Prince's residence, a *Schloss* on a cliff.

I was flattered, but not overwhelmed. There are, after all, a great many Film Festivals; the British Film Institute publishes a Directory listing some three hundred every year. However, it was true that I had never been to one. The London Film Festival hardly counts, since one reviews the entries as part of one's weekly stint, and Edinburgh is something of an exception; it has no Jury and does not award prizes. I wondered what the *lingua franca* of an International Jury would be; I speak a little French, but not enough to argue in it. I supposed that I was being asked because somebody else had dropped out. I supposed that the invitation had something to do with the Desmond person I had met at Academy Three, that he had been bruiting me about the Festival circuit as a true man of the cinema. Since it was Saturday, the bank was closed, but I went down to the Bureau de Change in the Old Brompton Road, and looked at the exchange rate for Swiss francs. Five thousand would be worth something like fifteen hundred pounds, which was nearly a third of what I could expect to earn in a year.

Monday of the last week of March would be the twenty-eighth, but one would have to travel on the Sunday, perhaps even the Saturday if there should be some sort of Opening Ceremony first, with champagne and speeches. I had heard that at Cannes the distributors gave lavish parties, sometimes several in an evening, at which starlets appeared with their nipples gilded, and although one despised that sort of thing, it would make a pleasant change; at Edinburgh, nipples, even of starlets, are usually covered by rainwear. Saturday the twenty-sixth was only five weeks away—yes, somebody must have dropped out. As I had told the Desmond person, the *Radical* has never been able to afford to send me abroad, but I had no doubt that my editor would welcome a despatch from Liechtenstein if my expenses were to be paid by someone else. I would be able to see most of that week's releases early, at Magazine Showings or Television Screenings; it could all easily be arranged. Only Bonzo would be a problem.

'What do you think, Bonze?' I said. 'It's a lot of money. I'd like to go.' She put her nose between my knees, and stared up at me; she could communicate emotion, but not opinions. Her nose was moist and black, and her eyes were brown, with amber flecks. I thought again how beautiful animals are, even those much older than she, while human beings . . . I thought again of the four naked, middle-aged men, and found myself shuddering. I said, "It's only for a week. You'd have to stay in a Kennels.' She pricked up her ears but this was because she had heard, far below on the ground floor, the front door slamming. The Australians were not in the habit of closing doors quietly.

I wondered whether my wife would look after her, but it would not do; there was a coolness between them. Bonzo would be happier with a man, but I knew none well enough to ask. Perhaps there were Boarding Kennels which specialized in alsatians. I would look again at the advertisements in *Our Dogs*. My wife said, 'It sounds very odd to me. What sort of Film Festival?'

'Something to do with an advanced developmental aesthetic. There is a brochure, but it's all in German.'

'Let me have it. I'll get it translated.'

As I had grown less directive, my wife had become more so. It was a consequence of being in charge, of course—a habit of command: one understands that. Nevertheless it annoyed me. I said, 'You needn't bother. I'll take it to the office.'

'The *Radical*!'

'We are internationalist, you know. We're committed to Europe.'

'Don't be so stuffy, Paul. I can't bear you when you're stuffy.'

There was a silence, during which both of us remembered that this was how the break-up had begun. My wife said, 'What will you do with Bonzo?'

'I thought a Kennels. I've been looking at small ads. There are places which specialise in the larger dog.'

'Dobermans?'

'Not necessarily. I'd want to visit the place first—look around and talk to the people. I wouldn't leave her anywhere I didn't think she'd be happy.'

'Do you want to borrow the car?'

'Could I?'

'You heard me offer.'

I recognised the note of impatience. During our last months together, there had been almost nothing I could say or do which did not inspire it. I said, 'Sorry. I was only making noises really. They meant, "Thank you".'

She blinked, and I thought for a moment that her eyes were moist, but all she said was, 'Humble bugger, aren't you?'

I suppose it is possible that she had been feeling some anxiety on my behalf, and that this had made her edgy. I said, 'You could get the brochure translated for me if you like. I'd be very grateful, in fact. We do take *Stern* in the office, but I don't think anyone reads the text.'

'Who would have thought that the pure love of an alsatian bitch could work such a change in a man? You get the cognac, and we'll have some music, and put our feet up.'

This indicated to me, but I hoped not to anyone else, that she intended to talk about the negatives. I said, 'Do you know, the police found a bug in the flat?'

'What?' My wife put down the Pergolesi, and reached for

something more noisy. Her hand lighted on *The Prince of the Pagodas*, which is not one of my favourites.

'It was behind a picture. Amazing! He found it with a sort of bleeper thing.'

'Why should anyone bug you?' my wife said, a little too loudly, I thought. She began moving quietly around the room, looking behind pictures.

'Don't know. Must be something to do with that man who was killed, but all I did was take his dog for walks. I don't regret that; I never shall.'

My wife picked up a reporter's note-pad and a pencil from her desk. 'Are you getting the cognac or not?' She wrote on the pad, and showed me the page as I handed her a glass. 'WHAT WILL YOU DO WITH NEGS?'

I had already considered this question, and had decided that the negatives would be safer left where they were, in Bonzo's collar, even at a Kennels, than on my own person or in any hiding-place about the flat. But I thought it wiser to lie to my wife, since I already regretted having told her where I had found them.

'HIDE THEM WITH OTHER HOLIDAY NEGS LIKE E. A. POE PURLOINED LETTER.'

'I'VE GOT MORE NEGS THAN YOU. BETTER LET ME LOOK AFTER.'

'NO!' I had been right to lie. My wife never gave up.

If two people are supposed to be in conversation, prolonged silence may be almost as suspicious as what is said. I told my wife to lie back with her head on my chest and get comfy while we listened to the music. *The Prince of the Pagodas*, I said, was always worth one's full attention.

So we listened to the music, and finished our cognac, and later burned the piece of paper on which we had been writing. My wife's flat was centrally heated, so we had to use an ashtray, and flush the ashes down the W.C. before going to bed. One feels such a fool, doing that kind of thing.

* * *

Most of the brochure turned out to be an essay by Professor Serge Bouclé, Professor of Cinematography at the University of Dieppe, who was to be our Chairman. It was written in the usual style of French academic criticism, which is exceedingly abstract, and translating it from French into German, then from German into English, had done nothing to make it more concrete. The professor informed us that, to understand the film of the Future, it was not enough to embrace the Shock of the New; we must renegotiate our concept of modernity altogether. The dialogue of a film was, of course, with its public, and also, equally of course, with its makers, but most of all with the dynamic dialectic of Film itself, which it would be most useful to regard as a web of glittering action. If that web should ever succumb to stasis, then the degeneration which had already eaten away the heart of literature and all the other *bourgeois* arts, etc, etc. Very early I began to skip.

What I had taken to be stills were in fact scenes of Liechtensteinian life—visitors buying blocks of newly-issued postage-stamps at the Official Philatelic Centre, skiing at Malbun, the assembly-line of the false-teeth factory at Vaduz, the church of Triesenberg in mist, and what I had guessed might be from yet another re-make of *Dracula* was simply labelled 'Ruined Schloss in Woods'. There was no hard information about the films in competition, except that there would be entries from the U.S.A., United Kingdom, Sweden, Denmark, Holland, West Germany and Haiti, and that further films of specialist interest could be viewed *hors concours* on videotape cassettes in the privacy and comfort of one's hotel room. There would be a prize, the Golden Pillar of Vaduz, a burnished column springing from boccage, and there would be certificates for entries which the Jury should declare to be of Special Merit.

Certain criteria had governed the acceptance of the entries, Professor Bouclé wrote: each should be of the utmost elevation, should extend the human capacity and enlarge its dimension. The International Jury would take no account of mere linear narrative; its judgement would be essentially conceptual. Well, we should see about that. I have something of a preference for mere narrative myself.

None of this told me what the theme of the Festival would be. I looked through the B.F.I. Directory, which among its various classifications of Film Festivals has one by subject, and found Archaeology (Verona), Architecture (Bordeaux) and Agriculture (Zaragosa). Perhaps in view of the brochure's many references to culture and concepts, Liechtenstein's would be Anthropology. Perhaps there would be an anthropologist, someone like Desmond Morris, among the Jurors. Perhaps it was Desmond Morris who had dropped out to let me in.

I did not care. I was looking forward to going. I raised my stock considerably at East Hounslow by informing the Department why it was necessary for me to be away on Friday, April 1st. I warned my class, told them that they should spend part of that week researching locations for our project, and meet at the usual time for a group-discussion under an elected chair-person. I ordered traveller's cheques and a little Swiss currency from the bank; though my expenses were to be paid, there were bound to be some extras. My wife took me to Harrod's, and bought me a shirt, a tie, and a pair of shoes. My evening clothes, although twenty years old, had hardly been worn, and still fitted me. The same was true of my only suit.

An air-line ticket arrived from a travel-agent in Twickenham. I was to travel on Saturday the 26th from Gatwick to Zurich by Falcon Tours: they might be generous with honoraria, but were economising on the flight. At Zurich I should be met. A single room with bath *en suite* had been reserved for me at the Statler Hotel in Vaduz, where my distinguished colleagues would also be staying. I supposed that I would be paid when the judging was over.

I borrowed my wife's car, and drove with Bonzo into the Cotswolds, where there are Kennels catering for the larger dog. We visited three. All seemed to be run by women, the first by a woman who employed women, the other two by women in partnership. I do not wish you to misunderstand me. I myself prefer the company of women to that of men; it was Bonzo who harboured misgivings. Nor did she seem to relish the propinquity of larger dogs. She had always been equable enough with other dogs during our walks together, had sniffed and allowed herself to be sniffed, but had lingered with none. At all three of the Kennels we visited, each larger dog was provided with space of its own for sleeping and eating, but there were communal areas for exercise. I watched dalmatians frolicking together, barking and hurling themselves enthusiastically against the wire-netting which separated us from them. It seemed to me that they were offering a welcome; I should certainly have recognised hostility. Bonzo laid back her ears, and growled. Later we were asked to admire the quantity and quality of raw horse which was to be fed to a labrador. I did so. Bonzo turned away.

At the third Kennels, she showed considerable reluctance to get out of the car. A sympathetic girl in wellington boots and a rubber apron said, 'I suppose she's grown up with men, hasn't she? A bitch gets fixated.' I asked whether the girl knew any men who ran, or were even employed by, Kennels for the larger dog, but it seems that, lacking the dedication, they are thin on the ground. I drove away sadly, no further forward in my quest.

You are thinking, 'The man is mad. He will board Bonzo in a Kennels. Someone will open the capsule attached to her collar. The negatives will be discovered.'

I had not neglected this area of concern. Indeed, a part of me had wished the negatives to be discovered in just such a way, so that the burden of responsibility should be lifted from me. The secret would be out, and must be told, and by someone else, while I should be able to pretend, or at least try to pretend, that I myself had never opened the capsule, and had not known what was in it. But that gutless part of me was overborne by the stronger part, which had taken a decision, made a plan to execute it, and intended to go through with that plan. The negatives should remain where they were, but hidden, until my return. I had attached one end of the roll, still in its covering of tissue paper, to a small piece of Blu-Tack, had pushed the Blu-Tack down to stick to the bottom of the capsule, had affixed another piece of Blu-Tack on top of the roll, puting a coating of Super Gloo over that, and painted over it with metallic paint bought at a Craft Shop. I made a false bottom to the capsule. Within the remaining space, I placed a folded piece of card on which were written my name, address and telephone number, and the offer of a reward if Bonzo were found and returned to me.

I had given myself a day to place Bonzo, and it was not yet over. There was a fourth Kennels at Sedgeberrow, west of Broadway, but my hopes of it were not high. Almost an equal distance to my north-east was Warmington, where Bonzo's breeder lived, Mrs Emily Stevenson. Since I had committed myself to the man in the brown suit, I should have put myself in touch with Mrs Stevenson at some time to enquire about a stud. Why not, being so near, pay a visit now? Perhaps she would know of a Boarding Kennels where Bonzo would be happy. Perhaps if she (and her husband?) had bred Bonzo, they might agree to board her themselves.

My visit did not begin happily. This time Bonzo's refusal to leave the car was positive; she would not be persuaded. It did not bode well. The house was a little way outside the village on the Mollington Road. A board on the door gave the time of Surgery Hours; the husband must be a doctor. A wooden arrow, on which were painted the words 'DOGS ONLY' pointed to a path leading to the back. I followed it. There was a lawn, various bushes not yet in leaf, wind-blown daffodils and tulips, the beginnings of a garden abruptly cut off by an expanse of high wire-netting with rough grass beyond it leading towards sprawling sheds of brick and wood. From the window of what must have been the Surgery, a woman watched me. She had red hair, piled high in the manner of a Toulouse-Lautrec poster, on top of a very white face. Her eyes were tragic. She sat at a desk, on which there were a typewriter and filing-cabinet. She did not speak or gesture, but only watched me.

I hovered, not knowing whether to approach the window or a gate which was part of the wall of wire-netting. From the sprawling sheds another woman apeared. Her hat, skirt and stockings seemed to be of tweed, her blouse of blanket; her boots were like boats. I opened the gate in the wire-netting, and went to meet her.

'Surgery's not till six.'

'I've come about an alsatian.'

'I've none for sale. I put a notice on the front gate when there are any.'

'You sold an alsatian bitch to a Mr Gavin Durston. It would have been . . .' How old was Bonzo? 'I'm not sure. She's not very old. I've got her in the car.'

'I don't take them back.'

'I thought you might have the pedigree. It's been mislaid.' The woman grunted. 'I thought you might give me some advise about a mate. I did ring the bell, but nobody answered.'

We were back in the garden. Mrs Stevenson padlocked the gate behind her. 'She won't answer. Not outside Surgery Hours.'

I was taken into the kitchen, and recognised immediately the smell of what had been fed to the labrador. There was a shoebox with cards in it on the dresser, and a large leather-bound book. 'I don't sell more than thirty a year. It's a vocation with me, not a business.' She tapped the book. 'Pedigrees go back a quarter of a century. All in coloured inks, you know. I spend hours.' She began to riffle through the cards in the box. 'D . . . Durston . . . No.'

'But I was told . . . positively informed . . .' It would have been most unlike the man in the brown suit to have made a mistake.

'Want me to look at her?'

We went outside to the car, and looked at her. Bonzo cowered away. The woman grunted.

'You recognize her?'

'Half a mo.' She had brought the book, and opened it on the bonnet of my wife's car. 'Hermiston Catriona Three? What do you think?'

'I'm afraid I've no idea.'

'Bloody Davey! No business selling her! Copied out the bloody pedigree from my bloody book, I'll be bound. Well, I won't take her back.'

'I'm sorry?'

'I don't deny she's one of mine. Hermiston Catriona Three by Champion Hermiston Alan Breck out of Hermiston Catriona Two. Mother died in whelp. Three in the litter. Two had pink noses, so *they* went.'

'Went?'

'Bucket. My own fault. Old Breckers was past it, I knew that, and anyway the bloodlines were too close. Greedy! You breed a real Champion, Best in Breed at Crufts, and you want to put him to everything. Never does.' She looked at Bonzo. 'She should have gone to the bucket as well, but Davey took her. Brought her up on the bottle. Said he wanted her for company, lying sod. Must have sold her. Do anything for money. Sell his mother.'

'Davey?'

'Used to help me out sometimes. Cleaning out. *She* wanted him for the garden. I wouldn't have it. "You can't serve God and Mammon, Davey," I told him, "Not both at once." "I'd serve a goat," he said, "if it'd pay me." I let him go. He'll come back when I want him. Sneaking in here, copying the pedigree out of my book!' She turned her attention again to Bonzo, who had left the passenger-seat, and was attempting to become one with the gear-lever. 'No point in mating her. Bad blood. Get her speyed. What did you say your name was? I'll put it on a card.'

She went back inside her house. There seemed to be very little point in asking her to accept Bonzo as a lodger, since it was clear that Bonzo would not lodge. I had brought a copy of *Our Dogs* with me, and consulted it. There were several Kennels in the vicinity of Coventry, though the larger dog was not specified. I started the car, and moved on towards the next village.

We had driven about a mile when Bonzo began to whine excitedly. We passed a turning. She barked, and, when I did not stop, attempted to jump through the glass of the window. I braked. She licked my face, and whined again. 'What's the matter?' She tapped at the door with her paw. I reversed carefully (it is not my greatest talent) until we came to the turning we had passed. Bonzo barked encouragingly. We turned left, and went up a hill, while Bonzo continued to make small whining noises of encouragement.

In this way, guided by my dog, I took one turning, then another, left the metalled road and drove along a rutted and muddy track, over a cattle-grid and down the hill to a cottage where, digging in the vegetable patch accompanied by two Jack Russell terriers, was a man of about my own height with hair as grey as mine. As we approached, Bonzo set up a mingled yelping and whining. I stopped the car outside the cottage, and leaned over to open the door on her side. She was out at once, and through the gate, jumping up, licking the man, and embracing him with her paws, while the Jack Russells frisked about, entirely unaggressive, which is not the nature of the breed.

I got out of the car, feeling very low. It was clear that I was in no way part of this reunion. The man said, 'Hullo, Bonze. Found your way back, then, have you?' He was broader than I, and considerably younger, probably in his late twenties or early thirties. He must have gone grey very prematurely.

Davey had been the Assistant Headmaster of the village school. When the Ministry of Education had closed it down, he had not cared to make a move; he had been over-qualified for the job, and had taken it because it afforded him solitude, a country life, and considerable free time. Some village children still came to him for coaching, and the parents paid what they could afford.

I had not eaten all day. He gave me home-baked

wholemeal bread and potted rabbit, and offered his own elderflower wine, which I refused; these country wines are potent, and I had far to drive. I told him that I should need to board Bonzo for a fortnight, since, although I should be returning on the Sunday week, there would be Press Shows for three days, and I should not be free to collect her until Thursday. He said that would be ten pounds, payable in advance. It seemed reasonable to me, less than a Kennels would have charged, so I paid it. I wondered whether Bonzo would agree to return with me. Well, I should find out when the time came.

He had bought the cottage cheaply because it was derelict, and had restored it. He lived by selling what he produced and by odd jobs—occasional commissions for commercial artwork (very poorly paid), mucking out, harvesting, jobbing gardening provided that he was not tied down by regular weekly hours. He kept bees, and took the Jack Russells rabbiting. His own vegetable garden was singularly unlike those of other village folk. He grew courgettes, *mange-tout* and asparagus peas, asparagus itself, globe artichokes, salsify, endive; even his french beans were purple, and his potatoes had rose-pink skins and waxy flesh. In a little cobbled-together greenhouse, he would grow golden tomatoes for their looks and cherry tomatoes for their taste, with aubergines, capsicums and melons. There was a fig tree on the south wall of the cottage, still protected at this season against frost with a polythene sheet. On Saturdays he went round with his motor-cycle and sidecar, selling this produce, with his home-baked bread, his honey and his rabbit pâté (in returnable earthenware) to rich week-enders.

'No cakes and pastries. I won't produce what I don't approve of.'

'Mrs Stevenson said you'd do anything for money.'

'So I will unless it's against my principles. I won't keep chickens—ugly birds! But if the price is right, I'll do anything I can do, which is a lot. I'm a qualified man— Teacher's Training Certificate—D. Phil. Carpentry, simple accountancy, poetry—I'm a published poet, though, mind you, I publish myself. Consequently hand-printing—classy jobs on handmade papers with little flecks in them to prove they really are hand-made. Consequently, occasional paper-maker; one thing leads to another with me. Decorating and plastering. Country crafts—well, just corn-dollies actually, which is a racket; trouble is, there's too much competition from the Women's Institute. I want to learn thatching, but the buggers won't teach it.'

'She said you'd copied Bonzo's pedigree from her book.'

'People who buy pedigree dogs want a pedigree.'

'How long did Bonzo . . . were you and Bonzo . . ?'

He looked at me. I wanted him to say, 'Don't worry. She'll come back to you when the fortnight's over.' He said nothing.

I said, 'You never feel the need for company?'

'If I want company, I go out.'

'Yes.' That was another difference between us. I had got into the habit of not going out, although, if I am to be truthful, after my wife left I had often wanted company. 'I'd like to read your poems some time.'

'They're for sale. Choice of three slim volumes, all first editions, hand-printed on hand-made rag-paper. Five pounds each.'

'I'll have one, then. The first; I'll start at the first. I'm afraid I have to keep some money for petrol on my way back.'

'Take three for the price of two. Ten pounds. I'll autograph them. You can get petrol by Access.' So he had twenty pounds from me altogether.

Bonzo accompanied me to the car, but did not attempt to get in. Davey whistled, and she trotted back to him without hesitation. I had so much wanted her to show a little hesitation. I turned the car with difficulty in the confined space, and started back up the hill. In my rear-view mirror I could see the two of them, standing looking after me. I beeped the car horn twice, and hoped it sounded cheerful.

I had no legal right to Bonzo, if Davey should wish to

keep her, but I would not give her up without a fight. I entirely lacked nobility. I would not resign my mistress to the better man.

What happened at Gatwick was strange. However, nobody complained about it in more than a grumbling kind of way.

I had taken the train to Victoria, and arrived, as instructed on the ticket, just over an hour early for the flight. I checked my suitcase, had my personal baggage scanned by those X-ray machines which make sure that one is not carrying firearms or bombs, and saw a notice in the Departure Lounge informing the passengers of my flight that we were to leave from what is called 'the satellite', a circular building at some distance from the Main Terminal, reached by monorail. I entered the single compartment of the monorail train. I was its only passenger. I did not lack conversation, however, for the train itself talked to me, telling me that it was built by Westinghouse and operated by British Airways. I said, 'How interesting!' whereat the train stopped, sighed, the door of the compartment opened, and I emerged into what looked like an Ice-Cream Parlour.

The circular room was divided into slices, with the Departure Gates at the rim, and the Duty Free Shops, Buffet and entrances to the toilets in the centre. The slices themselves were Waiting Areas, illuminated by striplights of coloured neon, a different shade for each slice. Thus the striplights for Gate 33 were light blue with a darker blue for Gate 34, purple for Gate 35, red for Gate 36, and so on. I observed that there was a small queue at the entrance to each of the toilets, and that a policeman was in charge of the Men's queue, a policewoman in charge of the Women's. When I reached the Waiting Area for my own gate, I saw two more policemen, one of whom directed me to the queue for men; the passengers of no other Waiting Area were being so directed. I put down my briefcase, since clearly it would be safe to leave it, with so many police about. 'Take your hand-luggage with you, please.' I joined the queue.

'What's all this about?' I said to the man in front of me, and he replied, 'Search me!' which was exactly what they did.

It was distinctly rum. Three men in white overalls, like butchers or hospital porters, had taken over the entire Toilet area. Only one male passenger was allowed in at a time. I wondered what would happen to the passengers in the other Waiting Areas who actually wished to use the facilities.

I was required to strip completely, and one of the men kept my clothes and personal baggage for examination, while directing me to go behind a curtain, where the second man stood ready to conduct a body-search. The third man remained by the entrance. His function would be to supply support and restraint should it be needed.

My hair was searched, and my ears; my eyes were examined for contact lenses. My skin was felt carefully all over. I asked what they were looking for, and was told it was drugs; they had been tipped off that a parcel of drugs would be smuggled on my flight.

The man ran a comb through my pubic hair, tugging at the knots. 'You're being particularly thorough,' I said.

'Have to be. Some of these hallucinogenics take up no room at all; you could sop your belly-button fluff in them. Foreskin back, please, sir . . . Right! Now lie flat on your stomach on the bed. Legs apart, please, sir . . . Right!'

'I hope you catch him after all this.'

'Oh, we've caught him already. One of the first. Sweated like a pig; you can always tell. French letter stuffed with heroin up the rectum. They don't realise, you know; these things can rot. Massive over-dose.'

'Then why—?'

'There's always the possibility, sir, that your first man's a decoy, and the main shipment goes with someone else.'

He stamped my right wrist with some kind of ink which would wear off, he said, after three days. I should not be allowed to board the flight without showing it, along with my Boarding Card. It is no wonder that the plane was an hour and a half late in taking off.

EASY VIRTUE

I WAS MET AT ZURICH BY A YOUNG MAN WITH A TWO-SEATER Maserati. The strangeness of the journey persisted; he was a strange young man.

His name was Franz. He said I must call him Frank, because his nature was frank. If he liked someone, he must speak out at once and say so, the same if he disliked someone; he could not pretend. Luckily he could see at once that I was his type, a sincere and thoughtful person; he was attracted always to the mind of a person, not to the physical appearance. He had much admiration for the English and their language, which was his own first language after German. He preferred the English cinema (by which he meant *Chariots of Fire* and *Gandhi*) to the German (by which he meant Fassbinder), and he himself read widely in English, both fiction and other works. He lifted my heavy suitcase from the airport trolley with an almost negligent ease, and stowed it in the boot of the car. For himself, he liked to work out at the gym sometimes, but that was of no importance; only the things of the mind were important.

I guessed that he could not be older than twenty-five, and might be as young as twenty. He was blond and as good-looking as if he had stepped straight out of an advertisement for expensive ski-wear. I could not tell whether he was German or Swiss, and he did not say; perhaps he was a Liechtensteiner. I attempted to discover what was his position in the organisation of the Festival, but he was evasive, saying no more than that the Director was very sincere and serious, and had some bad luck, so it was good to help him. I discovered to my embarrassment that I could not call him 'Frank', as he had requested; 'Franz' came out more naturally. He did not object to this, however; I had the impression that he would not object to anything.

We drove for some time beside a lake, which must have been at least fifteen miles in length, yet there seemed to be housing all the way along it on both sides. I said that I had not realised that Zurich was so large. Franz laughed his merry laugh. We had left Zurich long ago; this was—a name which meant nothing to me. I had believed Switzerland to be an essentially pastoral country, but it seemed to be as built-up as Torquay or the Côte d'Azur. I had expected snow, but Spring had come early, and already there were jonquils in these suburban gardens. As we drove on, the mountains began to crowd in on each side, and there certainly one could see snow and bare rock and the green of woods below. Franz changed down to overtake a lorry, and his hand brushed my knee. This had already happened several times, and, since I had not moved my knee the first time it had happened, I felt that I could not do so now without seeming to make a comment.

It was the strangest conversation. Franz appeared to have read most of my pieces for the *Radical* over the last two years, as well as my book on Pasolini, from which he quoted; it had been a major influence, he said, in his cultural development. I have always responded shiftily to praise, which discomforts me, even from people I respect. Consequently I would attempt to turn the conversation from my own work to the Festival, and somehow Franz would turn it back again. However, I gathered that there had been opposition to the sincere and serious artistic director, because most people in Liechtenstein did not have modern ideas; women in the Principality were not yet allowed to vote. I gathered that, because of this lack of modern ideas, money which had been promised had since been withdrawn, but that a sponsor had been found to take over the backing. This was all I gathered, except that Franz's own ideas were extremely modern. He had taken, when making a point in discussion, or when he wished to emphasise some piece of positive thinking, to placing his hand directly on my thigh. Finally I drew my raincoat over the area, and moved my leg.

There had been a second lake after the first, and then the river Rhine on our right. The valley grew narrower, perhaps only a couple of miles wide. We crossed the river. One section of ribbon-development gave way to another. I asked how soon we were likely to reach the Principality, and was told that we were already in it. There was a factory on the left. An undistinguished villa on the right was the registered office of Twiggy Developments. The road divided, and became one-way. A large modern church on the right, a palace of black marble and plate-glass on the left. Was it a Museum? An Arts Centre? No, the Post Office; I had been looking the wrong way, and had missed the Museum and the Art Gallery too. I had an impression of a great many Souvenir Shops, and then we turned off the main road just as it was about to link up with its other half and become two-way again. We climbed a little way, and stopped in the forecourt of an hotel. Before he removed my suitcase from the boot, Franz said, 'Do you like to take a sauna? There is one at your hotel. I am often there between ten and eleven in the evenings.'

He smiled at me, showing a set of excellent teeth. He resembled, I had decided, the young Horst Buchholz. It was impossible to misunderstand what he was suggesting. I came to the conclusion that he was from one of the production companies, making a bid for my vote. 'I'm afraid I only go in for Mixed Bathing,' I said. 'Please don't bother to carry my suitcase. I can easily manage it myself.'

When I unlocked and opened my suitcase, I found at the top, tucked into the plastic packing of the shirt my wife had bought at Harrod's, a duplicate of the small black object with which the man in the brown suit had located the bug in my flat. It was about an inch square, no thicker than a wrist-watch, with a circular indentation at what I took to be the front, and no visible controls but an On/Off switch at the side. Beneath it was a card which read 'With the Compliments of the Management'. There were two identical cards already in the room, one on a bowl of fruit, the other attached to a miniature bottle of champagne in a miniature ice-bucket which plugged into an electrical point by the bed.

This discovery put a new complexion on the incident at Gatwick. The object could only have been placed in my suitcase after I had checked in, and by someone with the authority and equipment to open the suitcase, examine the contents, and relock it, *videlicet* by those also responsible for the body-searches in the Toilets of the Gatwick Satellite. It seemed most likely, therefore, that their search had not been for drugs at all, nor need the other passengers of my flight have been put to such humiliating inconvenience, for it was only my own body which had required searching, in order that the colleagues of the man in the brown suit might be sure that I was not taking the negatives out of the country. 'With the Compliments of the Management'— well, that was his style, sure enough. He seemed to like one to know what he was about.

Did it also put a new complexion on the curious behaviour of Franz? No, because the man in the brown suit knew that I was not inclined that way. My first conclusion about Franz was still likely to be correct, that he was employed in some capacity by a production company with designs upon the Golden Pillar of Vaduz. When one considered the enormous sums of money disbursed by film-people on entertaining the Media—the hire of yachts and night-clubs, the mounting of floor-shows, the presentation of personalised fountain-pens—it was hardly likely that they would boggle at proferring complaisant company to an International Juror. After my remark about mixed bathing, I might now expect, I suppose, to endure the flattering attentions of some starlet, with or without gilded nipples. I hoped they would not have made her read my study of Pasolini.

Perhaps I might find protection in the company of my fellow-jurors. I must find out who they were and whether they had yet arrived, and introduce myself. An envelope had been waiting for me at the Reception Desk of the hotel, brown and thick and clearly official, addressed to me by name and with the comforting words 'English Language' at the bottom left-hand corner. My room was on the second floor. It had two beds, a small refrigerator, Musak, and a balcony facing an Alp; I had not yet examined the bathroom. On the Alp, the light was already fast fading, and dusk had reached the valley. I would have a bath, sip champagne, nibble at a grape, and catch up with the contents of the envelope. Then, well briefed, I would go down to fraternise with my distinguished colleagues.

I began to unpack, wondering whether I had brought enough underwear. It was odd that the man in the brown suit should believe that I might be bugged in Liechtenstein at a Film Festival. I switched the object on. It made no sound whatever. I weighed it in my hand for a moment, and then slipped it into the jacket pocket of the suit I would wear that evening.

A small plastic sachet of Badedas had been supplied free by the hotel. I lay in green and foamy water, breathing in the fragrance of what one is told are horse-chestnuts, pulled in my stomach muscles experimentally, let them relax again, and spent several eternities in the judicious contemplation of my knees, reaching at last the conclusion that, as knees, they were nothing either way.

The hotel towels were soft and large; one could dry oneself languorously, and I did. Still wrapped in the towels, I opened the miniature bottle of champagne, settled myself in the armchair, and turned my attention to the brown envelope. There was a programme; the screenings would begin next day, on the Sunday. I did not recognise the titles of any of the films, not even of the two British entries, though the name of one of the directors had a familiar ring. Was it to do with fashion photography? fringe theatre? television documentaries? commercials?—well, there were plenty of good people who had started in commercials. Besides myself and Professor Bouclé, there were three other members of the International Jury. One was Clinton Bard. I had heard that he had settled in Geneva; this would be a local event for him. Although he had not completed a picture for many years, his projects were always newsworthy; I was in reputable company. The other two were again names which I did not recognise, but since one was Yugoslavian, this was hardly surprising. Clinton Bard! It would be alright, the International Jury. French intransigence notwithstanding, with two English-speaking members out of five we should conduct our deliberations in the language of Sunset Boulevard, not the Sorbonne. I must remember to compliment Professor Bouclé on his English when we were introduced.

There was a pamphlet in the envelope, *The New Cinema*. I would dip into it over breakfast. Miniature bottles are finished surprisingly quickly. I decided to dress and go downstairs.

I was surprised to find the Reception Area of the hotel almost deserted, though it was well equipped for sitting about, with small tables of smoked glass, armchairs covered in suede, and a number of newspapers threaded into poles of polished wood. Apart from the desk-clerk, there was only a young woman doing tapestry, who looked up at me and smiled as I entered. The time was nearly nine o'clock. I had observed on my arrival that the restaurant was along a short corridor to the left of the desk, and faintly from it, now as then, I could hear muzak of *Snoopy and the Red Baron*.

I wavered. The young woman said, 'There's nobody in the Dining Room.'

'Ah!'

'They're all in the bar.'

'Ah! Thank you.'

The bar was to my right, insulated from the Reception Area by looped velvet curtains and a heavy door of decorated glass. I opened the door, and was assaulted by a cacophony of noise. There is a process by which, in order to be heard over other conversation, one raises one's voice, and others, in order to be heard over one's thus raised voice, raise theirs still more. This process can escalate. It had done so in the bar of the Statler Hotel. Over the general cacophony, I heard a man's braying laugh. A woman was shrieking—it could not be rape; it must be hilarity. Some of the nearer faces turned towards me. I had a confused impression of noses, large noses with enlarged pores, of facial hair, burst capillaries, heavy spectacles of various shapes, of sweat, most of all of sweat. I closed the door again. The young woman said, 'Can't face it?'

'Not really.'

'Nor could I. You with the Festival?'

'Yes.'

'So am I.'

'Do you think we should have something to eat?'

She indicated the glass door behind me. 'Jerry's in there somewhere. Jerry looks after me, when he remembers. We were going to take a look at the town, but it's business first with Jerry.'

'What sort of business?'

'Deals.'

'I'll look at the town with you, if you like.'

She paused in mid-stitch to consider my suggestion. 'Jerry—'

'They seem to have settled in for the evening.'

'I'll get my coat.'

Clinton Bard arrived while I was waiting for her. He wore a fur coat and a beret, and was followed by a driver carrying leather suitcases. I wondered whether I should introduce myself, but he took no notice of me, signed in hurriedly, and headed left at once for the restaurant, where *Snoopy and the Red Baron* had given way to a recording of *Green Door* by what seemed to be a German singalike of Frankie Vaughan. Most of the Statler's usual clients, I concluded, had been in their carefree twenties when these songs were current. Dinner at the Statler would be like a dip in the Fountain of Youth.

The young woman had put away her tapestry, and put on a belted overcoat of dark blue barathea, buttoned to the throat, and a headscarf. She looked like Julie Andrews; I found myself enormously reassured in her company. From the restaurant we could clearly hear the voice of Clinton Bard, thickened with rage, instructing the *maître d'hôtel* to take away this crap and bring him caviar. I said, 'I don't think Vaduz is very big. It seemed to be mostly Souvenir Shops. And the Post Office, of course.'

'There has to be a cinema. We ought to look at that.'

As we went out together, we could hear Clinton Bard telling the waiter, 'There will be very thin toast. There will *not* be chopped onion.'

Her name was Prudence Baines. The tapestry was from *The Mary Poppins Tapestry Book*, bought from a special shop in Sherborne, Dorset. She owned all the Mary Poppins books, and the records, and many marketing spin-offs (face-cloths, tea-towels, matching sheets, a loofah), and a video-cassette of the movie. Pru had a special affinity with Mary Poppins, she told me, because of having trained as a nanny before her resemblance to Julie Andrews led to her taking up an acting career. It was quite difficult to copy tapestries from a book; beginners would usually buy a canvas with a design in colour already printed on it. The shop in Sherborne sold only materials concerned with the art of tapestry—canvases, coloured wools, helpful literature, no rubbish.

We stood together outside the cinema of Vaduz, regarding it critically. It was a building in the Swiss style, covered in yellow stucco, with a projecting roof of red tiles, and a small cosmetic bell-tower which contained no bells. It stood at a junction of the one-way system with a side-street, abutting the Old Castle Inn, formerly the Schloss Blick; on the other side, an exterior staircase of open cement treads with a wooden baluster led to the projection-box. It resembled no cinema Pru and I had ever seen before, and I have seen cinemas in Lanzarote and Lemnos. High on the wall which faced the side-street, someone had painted Perseus confronting a dragon. Perseus rode a white horse, and carried a sword of flame. He was separated from the dragon by six feet of yellow stucco and a drainpipe. Perseus was wearing a cloak of corrugated iron. The dragon appeared to be suffering from engine-trouble. They were clearly wise to maintain a cautious distance.

At the front, concrete steps led up to an arched doorway, in which there was a plain door of light wood with a fanlight above it. Curving round the doorway was a design of hearts, flowers and fruit in black and orange over white stucco. It reminded me a little of decorative early Picasso, Pru of a numda rug. There was a glass display-case for stills to one side of the door; but there were no stills in it, only some kind of announcement in German which we assumed to be about the Festival. Above it was a concrete window-box, and above that another wall-painting, but this was of a woman. She carried a torch, had an owl on her shoulder, and stood on a scroll containing the one word, 'KINO'.

'Is that her name? Kino?'

'It's the goddess Athene.'

'You do know a lot,' Pru said. 'I've always respected knowledge.'

We were not alone. An old woman in black sat on a portable stool on the cinema steps, blocking the doorway. We had said 'Good Evening!' to her, which had brought no response, and since neither of us knew the German word for 'evening', and 'Guten nacht!' sounded more like a farewell than a greeting, we tried to behave as if she were not there, insofar as we could do so without disrespect. The old woman had a placard propped up by her side, but again the words were in German, and we could not understand it. As we were about to move away, she spoke. It was clear from her tone that we had committed some fault.

'What did we do?'

I said, 'Maybe it's a charity. They sit on the steps, and ask

for money. Nuns do it. We should have given her something.'

'I thought that was outside churches.'

'Yes, it is. Anyway I haven't got anything smaller than a
fifty-franc note.' I raised my voice to the woman, mimed,
and spoke distinctly. 'Sorry. No . . . change. English.'

'Wait.' Pru found a five-franc piece in her bag. Over one
pound fifty still seemed rather a large sum to give to a street-
collector. There was no collecting-box; one couldn't be sure
that the woman's placard represented any authorised charity.
However, Pru proferred the coin.

The old woman spat on it. Then she knocked the coin out
of Pru's hand. It bounced from the steps to the pavement,
and rolled into the gutter. Luckily there was no grating, so
that I was able to recover the coin. A light rain began to fall,
and we returned to the hotel for dinner in the restaurant, a
rather draughty proceeding, since Clinton Bard had broken
a window by throwing through it the pot of lumpfish roe
brought to him as a substitute for caviar. I dislike talking
about myself, so we conversed about Mary Poppins, about
the care of young children and the foibles of their upper-
middle-class parents, about Eaton Square and its environs,
which Pru knew well, and about Julie Andrews, whom I
had met once at some kind of function and Pru had never
met at all, but for whom she was so frequently mistaken.

We spoke very little about Pru's life as an actress. I was
curious, of course, but it is easy to be tactless when
conversing with an actress whose work one cannot remember ever having seen; if she had been well-known, I, of all
people, would have known of her. There would have been
long periods out of work. There would have been small
parts in films or on television, important to her, entirely
unmemorable to anyone else. Her training had been only as
a nanny; there had been no period at drama school. She
spoke of the difficulty of advancing one's career if one were
not prepared, as she was not, to make artistic compromises.
Dear Prudence! She was so common-sensical about everything else; I would not press her into the quarter-truths and

113

exaggerations by which actors preserve a self-image far removed from reality. I assumed that her presence at the Festival was as a dependent of some sort to Jerry, but Jerry was still in the bar, and we did not speak of him.

The telephone by my bed rang early, and a voice asked me if I would join the rest of the International Jury at breakfast at nine so as to get acquainted. Since our first showing was to be at eleven thirty, that seemed to be time enough. I decided to wear a jacket and tie. Some degree of formality might be expected of an International Juror, and if we were required to walk from the hotel to the cinema, the journey might be chilly, nor could one be sure that the cinema itself would be heated.

Downstairs the Reception Area had been transformed, as if in one of those fairy stories in which teams of industrious pixies labour all night. The suede chairs and coffee-tables of smoked glass had been moved out, and had been replaced by two counters and three large trestle-tables. One of the counters was labelled 'ACCREDITATIONS', the other 'INFORMATIONS'. Behind them on high stools sat girls in angora. Two of the three trestles had been covered with press-releases in various languages, and on the third there were six typewriters. An arrow, pointing to what had on the day before been a pantry for the service of coffee and patisserie, read 'STILLS'. Once again I was grateful for the internationalism of the language of film publicity.

There was a busy traffic of journalists, in roll-neck sweaters or serious T-shirts, between the counters and tables, and a hum of German conversation, cut here and there as if by a buzz-saw with Italian and decorated with the graceful upward inflections of French complaint. A large notice-board displayed a list of persons attending the Festival with their addresses in Vaduz; almost all of them seemed to be staying at the hotel. Pinned to the board also were photostats of articles about the Festival which had already appeared in Swiss-German newspapers and an announcement in German, French and Italian that there would be a Table Ronde at two thirty in the cinema before the afternoon's screening, at which the distinguished members of the International Jury would be introduced to the Press.

The pigeon-holes by the Reception Desk, which might usually be expected to hold only room-keys and the occasional telex, had been converted to the use of accredited persons by the addition of an extra tier for those not resident at the hotel, and were already stuffed, my own among them, with glossy promotional material and invitations to *vins d'honneur*. The decorated glass of the door to the bar had been covered with a poster reading 'FESTIVAL CLUB'. It was as if, except for the cinema itself, the whole apparatus of the Film Festival, which is normally spread in any Festival town or city over several widely separated buildings, caravans, portakabins and the like, had all been concentrated into this one hotel.

My accreditation, a plastic card bearing my name and an old passport photograph, had already been delivered to me in the brown envelope. I had no reason to linger in the Press Room, except that I felt more comfortable among fellow-journalists than I feared that I should amongst my distinguished colleagues of the International Jury. I fingered the press-releases on the trestle-tables, drifted to the notice-board, and began to pick out and tuck away such fragments of information as were in a French I could understand. I was doing my homework, and was plucked from it by the Artistic Director, who came in search of me.

'Mr Hatcher? I am Peter Zeiss. We expect you at the breakfast table.'

'I'm sorry. I got distracted.'

'Yes?' Although it was only nine twenty of an overcast morning in March, the Artistic Director was already sweating copiously. Sweat ran down from his thinning hairline behind his tinted spectacles, and continued on down the sides of his nose to splash from his chin. I thought of Peter Lorre in *M*, but pushed the thought away . . . The Artistic Director, sincere and serious and admired by Franz, had experienced difficulties in mounting the Festival. On this first morning, it was natural that he should be nervous, and I had added to his worries by being late for our conference.

We proceeded to the Restaurant where, perhaps as a tribute to the Festival, the music-tape was now playing *There's No Business Like Show Business* in the original cast recording. The Artistic Director guided me to a side-table where jugs of tinned orange juice stood ready for pouring into plastic beakers; there were baskets of tiny foil containers of butter and jelly, and the rolls, like Gloria Swanson, could have been of any age. A waitress in green looked for a moment round the swing door which communicated with the kitchen, and the Artistic Director, quick as an entomologist, pounced upon her before she could scuttle back into cover, and ordered her to bring more coffee.

At the breakfast table itself, conversation was already in fluent progress between Clinton Bard and the good professor, and I was alarmed to discover that it was in French. Luckily the Yugoslav spoke only English and Croatian, and the fifth member of the Jury, a very old Italian, hardly spoke at all. I was told later that he had been a clapper-boy with de Sica, and now occupied a chair at Turin, but whether at the University or an Old Folks' Home was never made clear. Professor Bouclé addressed him persistently as 'Cher Maître'.

The coffee was excellent, and there was plenty of it. It was settled that the language of the International Jury should be English, but that Press Conferences should be conducted in French and German. All five of us would appear that afternoon before the Press, but Clinton Bard, who spoke German, French and Italian as fluently as he did English, having attempted in the past to raise money in all four languages, would bear the brunt of the questioning. It seemed in any case likely that Clinton Bard was the only one of us whom the Press would actually wish to question.

We agreed that we would not discuss the films in competition until we had been shown them all. None of us had seen any of them before, but the professor assured us that this was not surprising, since work which was truly in the modern idiom found it difficult, under present conditions, to get the right sort of showing, and it was to obtain recognition for the artistic values of such work that the Festival had been set up in the first place. Time passed. Sweat dried on the Artistic Director, and he began to shiver. It was suggested that we should rendezvous in the foyer. Transport had been provided and was waiting.

We were driven the half mile to the cinema in two Mercedes, preceded and followed by the Press, reporters on foot and photographers on motor-cycles. Other limousines carried Pru with someone whom I assumed to be Jerry, and the accredited persons who had filled the Bar on the night before—men in dark suits, men in silk suits, men in jackets of no known tartan, the thin men who propose deals and the fat men who conclude them, insecure ladies dependent on men and self-assured ladies accustomed to commanding men. Agents, distributors, producers, publicity persons, they were not colleagues nor the public; they were the insiders who set films up and marketed them; they did not make films, but for their profit films were made.

Again there was a light drizzle, and the red carpet which had been laid over the cement steps up to the entrance of the cinema was already squishy. The old woman in black (or someone like her) had been joined by five other women, with a priest and three nuns. The doors of Mercedes were opened. We emerged. Flash-bulbs popped. There was a television camera, hooded against the rain. I looked behind me for a moment. Across the road, across the car-park which lay beyond it, at the top of a flight of steps which led down from the upper one-way street and separated the Chic Shop from one selling *lederwear*, there stood a fat man in a trilby. He was gazing across at me, and when our eyes met, he shook his head reproachfully, and walked on out of frame.

The International Jury proceeded up the steps, led at a run by the Artistic Director. The women in black held up placards, which I could not read. One of the nuns began to ring a hand bell. A small boy (or perhaps a dwarf) whom I had not noticed before, swung a censer in which incense was burning. The priest intoned in Latin. I had been surprised to see a priest outside the cinema at that time of a Sunday morning, but now assumed that he had been brought along to preside over some kind of opening ceremony, and asked Clinton Bard, who was at my side, whether we were being blessed. 'Oh, my dear fellow,' he replied, 'we are all God's creatures.' We entered the cinema, where thrones of red polystyrene had been set up for us at the back of the auditorium.

At most Festivals, members of the public may pay to see the films on show, but the cinema of Vaduz was not large, and it became filled by the Press and other accredited persons. I assumed that the films would be shown again later for the public. We settled into our seats. There was a short introductory cabaret, at which the Artistic Director, who had begun to sweat again, welcomed us in German, and interviewed in Italian someone whose name I did not catch, but who seemed to have been the cameraman on the first of the films in competition. Then the lights went out. A disembodied voice made an announcement, again in German. Faintly from the outside I could hear the clanging of the hand-bell and a susurration of Latin from the priest. The film began.

It took me some time to realise that what I was seeing, shot in soft focus, highly enlarged and in exceedingly slow motion, was a tongue licking a clitoris to the music of an Oboe Concerto by Carl Philip Emmanuel Bach, and an even longer time and considerable camera movement before I further realised that the clitoris was that of Miss Prudence Baines.

I had never seen a pornographic film before. It was in some respects an entirely different kind of cinematic experience, in others much the same.

Certain conventions were different. We saw two films that day, and in neither of them were the devices of cinematic narrative used in any meaningful way. Regarded rigorously, there *was* no narrative, only a series of sexual encounters achieved within no sort of dramatic framework. No misunderstandings, no disapproving parents, no conflicts of class or religion kept the lovers apart; if you could imagine *Romeo and Juliet* reduced to one extremely extended encounter in Juliet's chamber, with perhaps a little necrophilia at the tomb to follow, you would have some idea of the principles of dramatic construction employed. '*Boy meets girl, boy loses girl, boy gets girl,*' had become, '*Boy and girl are contiguously placed. Boy has girl. Boy continues to have girl in various ways,*' and although there were variations on this theme, they were in the main variations of the numbers involved and the accessories employed, as '*Girl has several boys*', '*Nuns have each other*', '*Girl in black leather thigh-boots has elderly gentleman,*' '*Boys wrestle on rubber groundsheet*', etc. etc.

Nevertheless cinema has certain basic rules which continued to govern even what we were shown that Sunday in Vaduz. The nature of the camera is that it can only show what it can see. I discovered that pornographic films are not intrinsically about sex, that is to say they are not about sexual congress between partners, involving penetration and mutually satisfying orgasm, because during penetration, whether it be vaginal, anal or oral, the most involved parts of the human anatomy cannot actually be seen. Of the forms of penetration listed above, the makers of pornographic films seem to prefer oral, as being easiest to shoot, but in any case what finally has to happen is a withdrawal, a breaking-off of the joyful congress, so that the male orgasm can take place in the open, where it is cinematically at its most effective. There it can be photographed lovingly and at length, and worked upon thereafter in the labs and cutting-room. The orgasm of Pru's first partner, a Scandinavian gentleman, generously endowed, was almost indefinitely prolonged by mixing to the Fountains of Trevi and back again. It had been moved away from mere natural lust, and wholly transformed into art.

'That priest?' I said to Clinton Bard.

'It was certainly no blessing.'

'A curse? Bell? Book? I didn't see a candle.'

'Oh, they keep that for when they want to snuff you out altogether. Of course, that may come.'

'Ah . . . what are we going to do?'

'Our job?'

'It's just as well you're answering the questions at the Press Conference.'

I do not wish to be misunderstood. I no more disapproved of porno films than of any other films. I was already familiar with the critical literature. There is a view, originating at the University of Texas, that since all cinema is a form of voyeurism, therefore the ultimate extension of cinema, and its purest form, is the porno movie. If Professor Bouclé had expressed himself in those terms I should have understood him. I had been misled by all that stuff about the developmental aesthetic, the need to renegotiate our concept of modernity, and his constant references to the New. Pornographic art is not new; it is the oldest form of image-making.

Meanwhile I had agreed to be a juror, and I would stand by that agreement. The question remained; should I apply my usual critical criteria to these films, or attempt to evaluate them in what I conceived to be their own terms.

Truth to tell, I was in a state of shock.

It came to me that the reason for booking me on a charter flight had not been to save money, but to ensure that I could not walk out of the Festival and return to London without buying another ticket on a scheduled flight, and of course I had no money to pay for such a ticket. I reminded myself that I was an adult male, that I had enjoyed sexual congress both within and outside marriage, and that I was familiar, at least in theory, with most of the deviations from what I usually reminded myself not to think of as the sexual norm. Furthermore I was opposed to censorship in almost all its forms. There would be no question of my walking out. I badly needed the fee.

My thoughts and feelings during the first day of the Festival were a great muddle, and my memory of the day remains a muddle. As we went in to lunch, the Artistic Director said to me, 'Did you enjoy the film?'

'It was sincere,' I said. 'And serious.'

'You really thought so?'

'I truly thought so.'

The Artistic Director pressed my shoulder emotionally, as to a brother. At lunch our conversation was led by Clinton Bard, and was entirely about food.

The Table Ronde that afternoon was a surprisingly staid affair. We had been hissed when we emerged from the cinema for lunch, and the group of indignant persons with placards was much larger for the beginning of the afternoon session; I assumed that some form of *jihad* had been preached at the morning Mass. The six of us sat in a line on the narrow stage, the Artistic Director and Clinton Bard in the centre, with the professor on Bard's right. The Yugo-slav and I sat at opposite ends of the line, and the elderly Italian was on the other side of the Artistic Director. He spoke only once, when he uttered the word 'Caca!' sud-denly in the midst of one of the professor's more extended extempore passages, began to laugh, then had a fit of coughing, and was led off the stage and back to his polystyrene throne.

I waited for the barrage. I had been present at occasions of this sort before, although always among the inter-locutors. There would be questions about the circumstances leading to the withdrawal of subsidy, about the confidence trick played upon the government of the Principality, about the affront to the deeply held religious convictions of the good Catholic people of Liechtenstein. The liberal journal-ists would egg us on to denounce censorship; the conserva-tives would accuse us of corrupting the young (though in fact there were no young among the accredited persons, except for the journalists themselves). But in fact, when there are three people answering every question, all at length, and every question and its answer has to be translated back and forth between French and German, very little pressure can be applied; few questions get asked, and none can be followed up in any probing way. Much of what was said washed over me; even the French was often too fluent to follow. Sometimes my name would be mentioned, and then I would nod and smile in what I hoped was not too ingratiating a way.

I remember that the Artistic Director very handsomely refused to blame the Principality for withdrawing the Festival's subsidy. He blamed himself. (Clinton Bard made sympathetic noises at this point, and Professor Bouclé indicated the most marked dissent.) There had been a genuine misunderstanding in the use of terms; the fault was his own. When he had first broached the prospect, he had used the word 'modernism', when he might more properly have referred to 'post-modernism'. (Professor Bouclé considered the distinction throughtfully.) The leaders of the artistic community of the Principality were well-disposed to modernism, but they were not yet fully attuned to post-modernism, and they were not alone in that. ('No, indeed!' said Clinton Bard.) The Artistic Director had no intention of affronting the religious sensibilities of any person, but his own duty was to the cinema. He had been determined, and still was, to present certain masterpieces of the post-modernist cinema to the artistic judgement of the world. Luckily an alternative source of subsidy had been found. (Bard and the professor applauded both these last statements.) At this point, someone among the journalists should have asked the Artistic Director what his new source was, but there were ten minutes of back-up yet to come from Clinton Bard and the professor, all of it requiring translation, and since the questions were being taken in rotation, and some conveniently noncontroversial questions had already been submitted in writing, the moment passed. It is true that, before the Table Ronde was over, a gentleman in black worsted did get up, and shouted, and waved his arms, but he turned out to be Egyptian.

Pru's Press Conference, which was held that evening in

the Reception Area of the hotel, was much more lively. All the stills were gone by then. Even the stills of scenery were gone. The trestle-tables had been taken off their trestles and stacked to one side of the room, and the suede chairs had been brought back and jammed together into rows, and the journalists packed into them higgledy-piggledy. Pru sat at one end of the room behind a coffee-table. She was supported by Jerry, who was introduced as her Manager, and someone from the Promotion Department of Arts Gratia Artis p.l.c., the film company. Free champagne had been made available at the Bar (or Festival Club) by courtesy of A.G.A. for an hour before the Conference began, and would continue to flow for an hour after it, but some of the journalists from the small-circulation newspapers and a contingent of students from the Munich Film School who had somehow acquired accreditation were unaccustomed to such largesse, and unable to believe that the drink would not run out, so they brought bottles into the Conference with them, and passed them noisily to and fro.

This was, you might say, my own territory. I had promised to cover the Festival for the *Radical*; I had a right and duty to participate. I sat at the back and felt like an alien. There was great confusion. Reporters competed to be recognised, shouting, gesturing, standing on the seats of the suede chairs, and falling backwards onto the notebooks of those behind them. A television camera on a stand had been set up perversely in the middle of the room, and had to be moved after a while in order to shoot from another angle. One of the smaller students from the Munich Film School became entangled in its cable, while another vomited decorously behind what he took to be a screen, but was in fact the protective shielding of the Sound Engineer. There was a microphone on the coffee-table in front of Pru, and hand-mikes were passed (always too late) among the reporters by two of the girls in angora, providing the smaller student, who had disentangled himself from the television cable, with the opportunity of becoming re-entangled. I had met him while washing my hands before lunch. He was a chatty lad, a *déraciné* Indian from Kerala State, who wrote poems indiscriminately in German and Malayalam, and intended, he told me, to redraft cinematic grammar entirely in terms of the images of his boyhood.

Photographers crouched in rows, three deep at Pru's feet, illuminating her fitfully with their flashbulbs, as if they were practising to be footlights, but lacked the application to provide a constant glow. She had refused to be asked or to answer questions except in English. The reporters were not put off by this restriction. Those who could not phrase their own questions found friends to do so for them, and the mumbled consultations among such friends added to the general level of noise and confusion. Pru was asked . . . she was asked shameful questions, as it seemed to me, and each questioner seemed to encourage the next to go further. What did she think of when she was being screwed before the camera? Did she get any pleasure from it, or was it just a job? Was she married, engaged, going steady, living with a friend, and if so, how did he view her participation in these movies? If she would forgive the question, was she lesbian? Frigid? How many takes were usual in shots of intercourse? Had she been auditioned for the part, and did she herself audition her male partners? Had she undergone any special programme of exercises to prepare her for the Deep Throat sections?

It was all like that. It was worse than that. Only the Egyptian behaved in a civilised way. His anger at the Table Ronde had been due to his not having been able to understand any of what was said, but he was quite able to operate in English, and, having possessed himself of a hand-mike, asked Pru gravely whether she really believed that the post-modernist movement in cinema was likely to lead to any increase in human understanding, or whether she would agree with him that it represented an artistic dead-end. Pru replied that she thought we all had a lot to learn from basic human behaviour when it was artistically treated, and he smiled at her, and shook his head, and she smiled back.

I don't suppose she had ever given a Press Conference before. It was as if Ars Gratia Artis had put her up to be sport for the reporters. She was not diminished by the experience. She seemed to have decided, as Mary Poppins would have decided, that children who are impolite must be given an example of politeness. She declined to discuss her private life, but answered all other questions with great seriousness. As an actress, she did not allow herself personal feelings when playing a character, but concentrated on being that character, feeling *her* feelings, thinking *her* thoughts. She always discussed her character's motivation with the director before every scene. Truth to the character was her only consideration in undertaking any role; she would do anything her character would truthfully do, provided that it was treated in an artistic way.

By the end, she had mastered them. The confusion subsided. They ceased to shout and bubble. They had no more to ask. Jerry sat behind her, nodding and puffing at his cigar. The man from the Promotion Department glowed. Pru produced a paperback copy of Stanislavsky's *An Actor Prepares*, and began to quote from marked passages. Soon afterwards, the Press Conference was over.

Jerry, the Press, the man from the Promotion Department, they all felt the call of free champagne. The room emptied. Pru remained where she was, and so did I. We stared at each other over a waste of suede chairs.

She said, 'You didn't ask any questions.'

'I rather liked that Eygptian.'

'Yes, he was nice.'

I left my seat, and went to her. I saw that her face was flushed, and her hands still trembled.

'Did you enjoy my film.'

'I was a bit shocked at first.'

'But it was artistic?'

'Oh, yes.'

'I wouldn't do anything that wasn't artistic. God gave us our bodies. We have to make proper use of them.'

I said, 'How long will Jerry stay in the bar?'

'Most of the evening. He doesn't eat much. He says he couldn't respect a man who was a slave to his stomach.'

'I thought we might have a bath, and then go out to dinner. The guide-book says there's a restaurant owned by somebody who used to be a chef at Maxim's.'

'Alright.'

It seemed quite natural that we should go to my room together, and that when I had closed the door, and locked it, I should kiss her.

When one considers what I had seen her do on film, it was a very decorous love-making. She did not do any of those things to me, and I, since I could not be sure of being shot in soft focus, did not move my mouth below her navel. Our love-play was gentle and caressing. We did not bite, we did not scratch, we behaved, on this first occasion—you may mock me for saying so, but it must be said—we behaved reverently towards each other. Pru's lips were cool. She hardly sweated. She did not cry out, or speak, except that from time to time she would ask, 'Is that alright?' It was as if I were making love to a docile little girl. Whether I gave her pleasure or not, I could not tell, but when I came she said 'Oh!' in a quiet but satisfied way.

Afterwards we had a bath together, and then went out to dinner.

Over a salad of tinned asparagus tips with *radichio*, lightly dressed with what seemed to be Heinz Salad Cream diluted, I said, 'What is Ars Gratia Artis exactly?'

'A film company.'

'Making or distributing?'

'Both; I think. They do a lot with video-cassettes. Jerry says they're just beginning to exploit the market in Adult Cable. Poised for it. That's why we're here.'

'Have you worked for them often?'

'The names keep changing. I mean, mostly you work for the same people, but they keep changing the name of the company. Anyway I don't meet the front-office people. Jerry looks after that. I work with the director, and the crew, and the other actors.'

'The same director and crew?'

'They're all free-lance. Some of them specialise, so you see the same faces. Like, I mean, Eddie, the cameraman; he did that interview this morning; he's very well known in the field.'

'He's Italian.'

'It's a multi-national industry.'

'How many films have you made?'

She began counting on her fingers, but gave up.

'You can't remember?'

'They don't take long to make. You finish one, and start another.'

'Doesn't sound very artistic.'

Pru put down her fork. 'They haven't all been artistic.'

'I'm sorry.'

'You have to get started somehow.'

'I know. I'm sorry.'

It was going wrong. Whatever it was we shared, the easiness, the mutual liking and respect, was going wrong. Even the dialogue was going wrong. I had been working around to a particular question, and the scene was going wrong before I had reached it.

I said, 'I've had it easy all my life. Grammar School. University. Then falling into a job I liked. Of course, it isn't very easy now, because I'm middle-aged, and I haven't any money, and it looks as if the job's going to pack up on me. But I've never had to do anything difficult or unpleasant. One forgets.'

She looked at me, and picked up her fork again. I was winning her back to me. I said, 'The greatest actress there's ever been—Rachel; she went on the streets when she was young, to pay for lessons. She had the kind of artistic purity which nothing could soil.' This was not entirely an invention. It came into my mind unsought, and such felicities have their own kind of truth.

Pru ate an asparagus tip. I said, 'I couldn't help noticing on the end-credits. There was someone I knew. Assistant to the Producer, Gavin Durston.'

This had been another muddling event of this muddling

127

day, which I have not mentioned up to now because I could not find a place for it in the narrative. Somehow what I had been glad to leave behind me in London had followed me, if only as a reminder, to Vaduz. The connection with my own employment as a Juror could only be coincidental, but the conjunction of Gavin and pornography, when one considered the nature of those photographs, was clearly not.

'Gavin?' She considered.

'Young. Dark. Blue eyes. Probably gay.'

'There's a lot like that.'

'I wondered if he'd worked on any other films with you.'

She shrugged. 'Can't remember. I mean, I can't put a face to him. Is he a friend of yours?'

'He's dead.' The waitress took away our empty plates. 'I wouldn't say a friend. I only knew him slightly. He lived opposite me for a while. I used to take his dog for walks.'

'How did he die?'

'Suicide, I'm afraid. It was just noticing his name on the credits that surprised me. I thought he worked in advertising.'

'Oh, there's a lot of part-timers,' Pru said. 'I mean, for what *we* do, you don't have to have a union card.' The waitress brought rare Chateaubriand with *rösti* and a jug of Vaduzer wine. 'Of course I joined Equity the moment I had the qualifications. I always keep myself in benefit. I can get an acting job anywhere.'

There had been a small picket outside the hotel when we left. It had consisted of a young priest, two women and two heavy-set men in dark suits with white mufflers; they had held up their placards outside the windows of the Reception Area during Pru's Press Conference, and been turned away by an embarrassed porter. The side-streets of Vaduz are ill-lighted at night in March, but as we approached the hotel we could see that they were still there.

We had finished our beef, and lingered over coffee. Clinton Bard had come in with the man from the Promotion Department and a couple of accredited ladies, and had stopped to chat at our table. He had congratulated Pru on a sensitive performance, and said that if he managed to get his present project even halfway into the air, he would remember her, and she had blushed with pleasure and been almost unable to thank him. To cover the moment, I had asked him what, when he had so many irons in the fire, had induced him to serve as an International Juror, and he had replied, 'Anyone who can afford to subsidise a Film Festival can afford to subsidise a film. I would do more for less.'

There probably are taxis in Vaduz, but it would make no sense for them to ply for hire by driving round and round the two one-way streets, and since the night was pleasant and the distance short, we had decided to walk back from the restaurant as we had walked to it. Before the hotel, the picket was packing up its placards, covering them with bags of heavy-duty black plastic so as to keep them fresh for the morrow. The young priest saw our approach from some distance, and came to meet us, followed at a respectful distance by the rest of the picket. There was a van parked further down the road; I supposed that they had come in that with their gear, and would return in it to the sacristy. The priest stopped us just after we had passed the van, and began to address us in an agitated way.

'I'm very sorry. We don't speak German.'

The rest of the picket parted ostentatiously, two by two, so as to avoid our contaminating contact, and walked on past. One of the women spat. Clearly it was what women did in Liechtenstein, but, lacking the vote, how else could they show disapproval?

The young priest continued to address us in German. I said, 'The intention was artistic. That makes a difference. I'm sorry we can't stop to explain.' A heavy-duty black plastic bag was placed over my head from behind, and pulled down swiftly almost to my knees. I opened my mouth to shout, and it filled with plastic. I heard Pru squeak from beside me. I remembered newspaper reports of suicides and euthanasia carried out with plastic bags, but surely they were not heavy-duty garbage-bags, but of the sort used to protect expensive clothes from dust. There flashed into my mind a picture of Pru and myself, hanging up side by side in a wardrobe, our necks askew. Somebody was tying my legs, and as I began to struggle, another piece of rope over the outside of the bag confined my arms. I blew out, and prepared to shout again, and a hand pushed the plastic bag into my mouth, and kept it there while I was lifted off my feet and over a shoulder, to be flung into the van. Pru landed on top of me. The engine started. I tried for the third time to shout, and the van moved up the road. At least I supposed it was up. It had been facing uphill, and although, with one's head in a bag, one is not in the best position to estimate direction, we could tell that the road twisted because we were thrown about the floor of the van whenever it did so.

The rear door had been closed. None of the picket had got into the back of the van with us. There would be the driver in front, and probably a mate. These could be the two middle-aged men, or it might be that we had been handed over to the activist wing. It was dark, the same total blackness which had scared me into something like paralysis in the bathroom of the flat, but this time I was not alone. The movement of the van had thrown Pru off me, but I could feel her, as we bumped about against the sides of the van and each other. She would be frightened, and bruised like an ill-protected parcel. I imagined her sobbing. I wanted to touch her, and reassure her, but my arms were constricted. I said, 'Are you alright, Pru?'

A small voice replied, 'I'm afraid of the dark.'

'Don't worry. If we can rub the bags upwards against the floor, we might be able to get our arms free and then untie our legs.'

Somebody laughed. I heard a match strike, and after a while the smell of cigarette smoke began to make its way inside the bag. None of the picket had got into the back of the van, but I had forgotten that someone might already have been waiting in it.

After a little while Pru was sick. I could hear her, and smell the vomit. I feared that she might drown in it. I shouted. 'Do something, you bloody fool. Get that bag off her head, unless you want her dead,' and then, 'Pru, lie on your stomach, and try to keep your head up. Don't lie on your back.' Perhaps she would have been safe enough, perhaps even safer, on her side; I didn't know. I felt the bag beside me jerk itself over, and I heard a banging on the partition between the body of the van and the front seats, and then a man's voice speaking urgently in German. The van stopped, and I could hear the bag being removed from Pru. Then the van resumed its journey uphill, and it was I, lying there in the blackness, who was weeping silent tears, but they were of relief.

Will you believe I slept? I myself find that hard to believe, yet it seemed that suddenly the temperature had dropped and the van was bumping along an unmetalled road. Again the man was speaking in German, but this time to Pru, who must have understood the tenor, if not the matter, of what he said, and replied, 'Please don't put the bag over me. Tie something round my eyes.'

'Bitte?'

She must have demonstrated. She stood up, and there were sounds, but not of the bag.

The van came to a stop and the doors were opened. I myself had to be assisted to my feet, and at first found it difficult to stand. My legs were untied. I considered a swift kick in the hope of hitting a vulnerable part of whomever was doing the untying, but decided against it; they had used no violence towards us so far, and it would be unwise to initiate violence ourselves without a much better chance of advantage coming of it.

Getting from the back of a van to the ground when one cannot see the ground is not easy. Pru, blindfolded, seemed to manage it with help. I was not helped, and my arms were still constricted.

I fell into snow. It was virgin snow, not slush, not deep (or the van could not have negotiated the road), presumably it was what remained from the winter. We must have been taken above the snow-line, but not far above.

We were hustled a little way over snow, then up steps onto the wood of a porch, inside a building which, I was glad to discover, was heated. Up more stairs, then a carpeted landing, a second flight of stairs, six paces along another landing or hall, this time uncarpeted, into a room, left there, the door locked and bolted behind us.

Pru removed her blindfold, and helped me out of the plastic bag. The room was bare, lit by a single bulb hanging from the ceiling; the switch was by the door. It had windows, but the bars which kept the shutters closed had been screwed into the wood. There were two mattresses on the floor, each with a duvet. There was a card-table, with two canvas chairs, and on the table a pack of cards, two apples, a plastic jug of water with two cardboard cups, the *Reader's Digest English Bible* and a paperback novel, also in English, by Dick Francis. A screen in one corner concealed a thunderbox, on the lid of which they had left a roll of soft toilet paper. I supposed that in the morning our captors would bring us food, and water to wash, and would empty the thunderbox. Our confinement was to be spartan, but not rigorous.

I said, 'I don't think we need to worry too much. It looks as if this is just part of the Protest Movement. They're not real kidnappers; they won't be holding us to ransom, except perhaps to put a stop to the Festival. I'll try to do something about those shutters tomorrow.'

Pru said, 'I hope we meet someone who speaks English soon. We're going to have to find a way of telling them I'm diabetic.'

From outside we could hear the van start up and move off. Pru said, 'I'm supposed to have two injections a day, night and morning. I've missed the night one.'

'So what will happen?'

'I'm not quite sure because it's never happened before. I suppose I'll start to feel poorly some time in the early morning.'

Poorly didn't sound so bad. Feeling poorly is certainly something one can put up with in others. I had a headache myself, brought on by the staleness of the air in the plastic bag.

'Then I go into a coma, and after a bit I die.'

I stared at her. 'How long a bit?'

'I'm not sure.'

'How long between feeling poorly and going into the coma?'

'I'm not sure.'

I found myself suddenly savage. 'You're not sure of much, Pru.'

'I told you, it's never happened.' She began to cry. 'Some hours, I think.'

'I'm sorry. I'm sorry.' I went to her; I held her; I kissed her. There was dried vomit on her face and dress and in her hair. She was no longer the cool lady I had fucked so reverently. If you had asked me at that moment, I would have said I was in love with her.

I went to the door. I shouted. I banged on it with my fists and the light wooden frame of a canvas chair. I kicked it. There was no response, but whoever was in the house (if there was anyone in the house) would not respond anyway to bangs and kicks and shouts for help.

Would our captors have driven off, and left nobody in the house? Idiotic notion! The house was heated; there were carpets up to the first floor; people must be living here. I shouted, 'We need help. Somebody's ill.' I shouted. 'This is not a trick.' I shouted 'You've made a mistake. You could be guilty of murder.' There was no response.

In the movies of the thirties, people used to break down doors by charging at them, shoulder first, but a realism of detail came in post-war with the Italians, and made its way gradually throughout the industry, and nowadays those movie-actors who attack doors in that way only bruise their shoulders; an iron crowbar is required, or else one shoots off the lock. There was nothing in the room resembling an iron crowbar. I bruised my shoulder.

133

Pru sat on one of the mattresses, huddled up in a duvet. Energetic exercise would only use up the blood sugar more quickly; she must rest. I looked at my watch. The time was half past midnight. We had left the restaurant at ten. She would begin to feel poorly at some time in the early morning. How early was early?

There were three windows. I looked at the wooden bar which secured the shutters over the nearest. It had been screwed to the wood tightly, top and bottom, all the way down its length. The other two had been treated in the same way. I said, 'Is there anything in your handbag I could use as a screwdriver? Scissors or anything? A metal nail file would be good.'

'I dropped my bag when they attacked us.'

'We'd better have a think.'

I considered all the objects in the room. The chairs and table were flimsy. Cardboard cups and a plastic jug. Water. Apples. A Bible and a paperback—Dick Francis is notoriously good on detail, but it was unlikely that we would have been left a story containing instructions on how to break out of a locked room using only a pack of playing-cards and two apples. Two mattresses with duvets. Well, they would be useful to break my fall if only I could get a window open, but their time was not yet. A thunderbox. It was solid enough, being of polished teak or elm or some hard wood, and the pot inside was of enamelled metal. If there was hope, it was in the thunderbox.

It was more solid than my shoulder, and would not bruise. Since there was no carpet in the room, and the floorboards were of varnished pine, I should be able, by starting far enough back, to get some momentum on it. I ran, pushing the thunderbox before me, the full length of the room against the door. At the first attempt, it stuck at a place where the floorboards were not level, and sent me sprawling. At the fifth attempt, the hinge came off the lid. Pru, still wrapped in the duvet, stood up to watch.

The door was dented, but no nearer opening. It was of solid wood; if there had been plywood panels, I might have broken through. I took the top of the thunderbox as the nearest thing I could get to a crowbar, and attacked the hinges. The hinges withstood my attack. I attacked the lock and the places where I thought the bolts must be. The lock resisted; the bolts resisted. I broke the handle on the inside of the door.

I returned to attacking the body of the door with the thunderbox. If there were anyone in the house, we must have been heard. Was there no householder to be affronted by the damage we were doing to his property? Any householder, any tenant should be made welcome, promised financial redress, and, if only he could speak French or English, made aware that one of his prisoners was a diabetic. I had believed that all the Swiss spoke English as a second language, but this seems only to be true of waiters, hotel receptionists and the business and professional classes. And surely householders? Please God, householders! 'Malade!' I shouted. 'Mademoiselle est malade. Danger de mort!' I was soaked and dripping with sweat, and my whole body trembled. The solid wood of the thunderbox crashed against the solid wood of the door. Nobody came.

Pru was by the furthest window. She said, 'I think one of these shutters is loose.'

She was right. When one pushed against the shutter, it moved a little. The bar (which I had already examined) was screwed securely across both shutters; they could not be opened in the normal way. But in the hinges of one side, where weather had rotted the wood, the screws were not secure. They would not withstand the top of the thunderbox.

Nor did they. One hinge went, then the second. The shutter flew outwards. I looked down, and could not see the ground, but I knew that we were only on the second floor, and that there was snow. If there were also a metal fence, or wire, or the spikes of farm implements, I should regret jumping, but there was no alternative, and two mattresses with two duvets, carefully dropped, should give me some protection, even against spikes.

For a moment the moon emerged from behind thick clouds, and I saw that there were no spikes, but only a stack of cords of wood piled up by the side of the house, which considerably decreased the distance to be jumped. The mattresses, duvets and my overcoat were sent first to prepare the way. I jumped, and landed safely on the stacks, then jumped again to the ground.

There were no lights in any of the rooms of the house, which was empty, the front door locked. I broke a window with my shoe, wrapped my jacket round my fist to knock out the shards of glass, and so proceeded professionally indoors to rescue Pru.

'We'd better walk until we get to the main road.' I had returned to the woodstack for my overcoat and a duvet in which to wrap Pru. 'I know it's late, but maybe there'll be something moving, and anyway we can keep walking until we reach another house.' I had not dared to leave her, in case it took too long to find help. The time was nearly two o'clock. How early was early?

We heard the lorry long before we saw it. I stood in the middle of the road, my arms held out, my overcoat and jacket open to display my white shirt. The lorry-driver had to stop or kill me. Once again we had come across a Swiss with no English, or any language but German, but Pru stepped forward into the headlights to display her condition, and he knew an emergency when he saw one.

I wanted to go immediately to a hospital, but Pru reminded me that all the essentials for her injection were in her room at the hotel, so he drove us to the Statler. Since our captors had not been vulgar kidnappers, but religious persons acting in defence of principle, they had not robbed me of my wallet. We went through the pantomime of my pressing money on the lorry-driver and his refusing it, and he drove off well pleased with a fifty franc note.

Three o'clock. The journey had been faster down than up. How early was early? The night porter looked up as we entered, said 'Gruss Gott!' and gave us our keys, as if our appearance were not at all out of the way. As we reached the foot of the stairs, Pru said quietly, 'Give me a little time to get cleaned up, and then come to my room if you want to. I'll ring you.'

'The switchboard!'

'Internal calls don't go through the switchboard.'

'How are you feeling?'

'A bit funny. I'll be alright when I've had the injection. I want to thank you properly.'

Back in my room, I stripped and took a bath. I considered wearing pyjamas and a dressing-gown to go to Pru's room, moving suavely through the hotel corridors like someone in a sophisticated comedy, but my pyjamas are of winceyette and tie with a cord, and my dressing-gown is not of silk, or even of terry towelling, and there are egg stains on its lapels and Bonzo has chewed the hem, so instead I put on clean underwear, the masculine perfume from Harrod's given to me by my wife, and my suit. What gave me particular pleasure was that, if Pru could ask me to her room at this time of the morning, she was not sleeping with Jerry. The phone rang.

She had washed her face clean and pink, and smelled of Yardley's Lavender. I kissed her, and she tasted of toothpaste. There was a funny whistling noise somewhere in the room. I realised that it was coming from the pocket of my suit.

'What's that noise?'

'Just an alarm. I forgot to turn it off.' I hoped that my voice sounded casual enough not to alarm the listeners. I put my hand into my pocket, and switched off the little black plastic object.

Then I did a very foolish thing. Indicating to Pru that she should make no comment, I began to search for the bug. While I was doing so, Pru unlocked the door, and let the listeners in.

THE LADY VANISHES

THERE IS HARDLY A DEPARTMENT STORE IN LONDON WHICH does not post notices warning would-be shoplifters that they are under surveillance by hidden cameras. Even supermarkets have them. Should I not have realised that the listeners, once they had me in a place of their own choosing, would become watchers also?

There were three of them, Jerry and Franz and the young priest, who was not, of course, any longer wearing a soutane. Jerry sat down on the bed. 'Now you've done it,' he said. The young priest had one of those Swiss Army knives, and was using it to clean his fingernails.

So far I had always managed to find innocent explanations (usually connected with Bonzo) for my behaviour. But Bonzo was, at least temporarily with another master and content to be so, and Pru, whom I had for almost twelve hours loved more intensely than Bonzo, more than my wife, Pru for whom I had been ready to die in the middle of the road if the lorry had not stopped, for whom I would have thrown myself on spikes or wire, Pru had been the conscious agent of my entrapment, and this paralysed me; it dried up all my invention. I stared at the three of them, and could not speak. Pru had excused herself, and gone to sit in the bathroom. 'Put it this way,' Jerry said. 'You're not as simple as you look.'

The interior decorator had been beaten to death by a bit of rough he had picked up in a pub near King's Cross. The three men opened the door of the bedroom, and indicated that I should go with them. They took me to the lift. I should have cried out, resisted, but the young priest kept the point of the Swiss Army knife close to where I believed my kidneys to be located, and it seemed wiser to go quietly, at least for a while. Somewhere inside my head, whatever would eventually muster the spiritual resources to fight back was saying to me, *They do not know you have the negatives. They only know that you could tell you were being bugged.* The lift descended to the basement, where the hotel's Sauna was located. They opened the door to the Sauna, and conducted me inside. 'Now we give you a nice massage,' Franz said, and smiled.

I said, 'You're the people I was warned against, I suppose.'

'Who warned you?'

'The police.'

The Sauna consisted of three main areas. There was the enclosed sauna bath itself, with a shower and W.C., an area for massage, with a plunge bath, two marble slabs and a closet where the masseurs kept their gear, and a carpeted area, with wicker chairs and magazines, a telephone, and a pantry with an espresso machine and a refrigerator for cold drinks.

What was it about marble slabs that I should remember?

The negatives. My enlargements had been too fuzzy for me to be sure, but I had received the impression that the teenage victim had been lying on a slab of some sort, as in a mortuary. Or a Turkish Bath or Sauna.

They required me to strip. Even if my physique had been like Franz's, I should have felt vulnerable; wolves, which run on four legs, are all of a piece, but in humankind the male genitals hang about like expendable old men, left by the defending garrison outside the gate of the citadel to be slaughtered. I said, 'The police told me that there were people who thought I might have something belonging to Gavin. I don't have anything, and the police know that, but they said I'd have to be wary.'

'And you were wary. Too wary by half. Wandering about the room with that object!'

'Given to me by the police.' It was important that I should keep reminding them that the police had already interested themselves in my welfare. 'I haven't got what you're looking for. I don't even know what it is; I don't think the police know. Whatever you do to me, you can't get out of me what I haven't got, and the police will know it wasn't an accident.' I could read nothing in their faces, but I had to go on; I had to make some kind of convincing offer. 'Alright, I know who you are now; you're thinking I know too much already. You should have left well alone; you've landed us all in it.' No response, not even a defence. 'But we can come to an arrangement. You've done nothing so far but threaten me. Why waste your time, and put yourselves at risk, by trying to get something out of me which I haven't got? I didn't know Gavin, I only met him twice, and I never even knew he was a man until the night he killed himself. Let me go now, and I'll keep quiet about all this. It's nothing to do with me, and I've had as much as I can take of the police.'

It would have been a more convincing performance if my voice had not been shaking, but that might be considered appropriate under the circumstances, and I hoped that Jerry at least would respond to the logic of what I had said. The young priest began to sharpen his knife on the marble slab. Franz said, 'Please lie down on your back. We do the front first.' I did so. It would be even more difficult to establish any kind of dominance while looking up at them.

Jerry said, 'Put it this way. You answer a few questions, and we'll let you go. I can't put it fairer. What did Gavin give you to look after for him?'

'Nothing.' Franz struck the inside of my groin hard with the side of his hand, which caused me extreme pain, and I screamed. I had no hope of being heard. They would not have brought me down to the Sauna if it had not been soundproof. And marble slabs are easy to wash down.

Franz moved round to behind my head, and touched my shoulders experimentally. His hands smelled of sandalwood. One of my shoulders was already bruised where I had charged the door of that upper room. Idiotically, I almost asked him to be careful of it. He flexed his fingers, and searched for a muscle. This time I tried not to scream, so that he should not guess how much pain he was causing by even grasping that shoulder. My attempt failed. I screamed anyway.

'I told you I don't know anything. I haven't got what you're looking for.'

'That's for us to find out.'

'It's tender here, eh?' Franz said.

'I'll go back to the beginning. How did you come to meet Gavin?'

'Through his grandmother. She was a neighbour of mine.' I have almost no tolerance to pain, but as long as I kept talking, they would not hurt me; therefore I must talk for as long as I could without saying anything. Sooner or later, I would trip myself up, and then they would kill me, but they were probably going to kill me anyway.

I told them in considerable detail what I had already told the police. As I did so, Franz's hands left my shoulder and began to caress my chest, moving gently across and down and round, almost as if he were giving me a present for being co-operative. Like a lover, he stroked and felt my nipples and the skin around them, pushing it up between his fingers to make pseudo-breasts. While he was doing so he smiled down at me, then looked up and smiled also at the young priest, whose expression was sullen and disapproving.

'And what did Gavin give you to look after for him?'

'Nothing.'

The pain again. It was more than I could bear, and Franz had done no more than take my nipples between his fingers, squeeze hard and twist. This was only play to him; he had not yet begun the business. His fingers released my nipples, and began, gently again, to explore the glands in my neck.

Jerry said, 'You're not a stupid man, Mr Hatcher. You know perfectly well that, if Franz was to go too far—broken bones, major internal bleeding, anything of that sort.' The loving smile seemed to have been pasted onto Franz's face.

His thumbs pressed a little harder into the glands of my neck. Thyroid! I had seen women with thyroid trouble, their eyes sticking out as if growing away from the sockets. Could one bring such a thing on by manipulation? 'Even if that should do the trick, we'd have to finish you off—in a humane way—because something like that, it'd be a hospital matter; it couldn't be covered up.'

'You couldn't explain a body either.'

'What body? You were never here.'

'The Night Porter saw us come in.'

'Nobody saw you come in.'

'The lorry-driver who gave us a lift.'

'That driver had been waiting patiently up the hill for you to escape. He says you took your time. Try to get this through your head. If you make us kill you, then you'll be taken back to that house up the mountain, and as far as anyone will be able to tell, you'll have had a nasty accident trying to escape from a posse of Vaduzian vigilantes, who will never be discovered because the people round here are a clannish lot, and they disapprove of you anyway.'

'Pru was with me.'

'You were alone. She hasn't got diabetes either. That was just to make sure you'd try to escape. You might have been tempted to wait it out otherwise.'

I closed my eyes. 'She was sick in the van.'

'She gets car-sick.'

Tears trickled from behind my eye-lids; they were of self-pity, but would be taken as evidence of fear. I said, 'You've been to a lot of trouble.'

'You're a lonely man, Mr Hatcher, mostly on your own, nobody to talk things over with. We thought we'd give you someone to trust and confide in, but with only a week to get acquainted, we had to make sure you got very close very soon.'

'We were close already.'

'There's nothing like saving someone's life to bring you closer.' It was clear that he was disappointed in me. 'You could have spent whole nights together. Pillow talk! You'd

142

broached the subject already; she'd have had it all out of you. How could we have known you'd be carrying that bloody object?'

'Given to me by the C.I.D. They won't believe in your vigilantes. They'll guess what's happened.'

'Doesn't matter what they believe; they've got no jurisdiction here. The local police will believe it. That's why we got you out here in the first place.'

'*You* got me out here?'

'On the Jury. Who the hell else do you think would pay you to judge so much as a Village Flower Show? So what did Gavin give you?'

'Nothing.'

Pain.

'You're lying. He gave you his dog.'

'The dog came to me. Then I kept her because he was dead.'

'Why? You say you hardly knew the man.'

'I knew the dog.'

Pain.

Jerry said, 'Make some coffee, Dieter. We'll give Mr Hatcher a moment to think it over.' That told me something about the pecking order. I could not be certain whether Jerry or Franz was in charge, but clearly the young priest ranked third.

Franz took his hands from my throat, and repositioned himself. Again he was like a lover, caressing and stroking. He, I supposed, would have had Pru's part to play if I had been that way inclined. Perhaps he was showing me what I had missed. His hands moved now as delicately as butterflies on my belly. His fingers circled my navel, stroked my lower ribs and the insides of my thighs, investigated my pubic hair, playing with my penis like a cat with a mouse, lifting and dropping it. He slid one hand under my scrotum, and held it, cupped. Just so, in the film, had Pru held the scrotum of the Swedish gentleman. It was the tenderest promise of what would happen to me next time I answered, 'Nothing.' I felt my genitals contract spasmodically, and almost pissed myself with fear.

With one bound, Jack was free. There must be something I could do or say which would alter my condition for the better. All I could think of was that there had been an error in the Natural Order; it was my job to write about characters in extreme situations, not to be one of them. Had the interior decorator thought such thoughts? He had known nothing they wanted to know, owned nothing they wanted to have, but they had beaten him to death anyway.

I said, 'It won't work.' The hand tightened its grip on my scrotum, and I began to speak quickly. 'Pru and I left the restaurant together. We were seen there. If I'd been kidnapped under her nose by Vaduzian nutters, she would have raised the alarm at once.'

There was a silence. Franz's grasp was still firm, but he did not squeeze, and he was no longer smiling. He said, 'He is right. Maybe we should leave the girl there also. I will get instructions.' At the door, he paused. 'Nutters?'

Jerry was unhappy. 'Mad people.'

'Yes. They would have raped her first, and then beaten her to death.'

The young priest said, 'That is correct psychology. The good Catholic murders the prostitute with whom he has sinned. It is often done.'

The telephone began to ring. They were all three startled, clearly not expecting it. Franz took a step back into the room. I felt it safe to turn my head. The telephone continued to ring, and then it stopped.

I made an effort; one has to make an effort. 'I told you they were keeping an eye on me.'

Franz said, 'There is an internal switchboard. Someone has dialled a wrong number. I will get instructions about the girl, and return.'

Franz was in charge then, not Jerry. Moreover Jerry was unhappy at the turn events had taken, and all three had been a little disconcerted by that telephone. I began to feel a small return of courage. Because of the tripartite division of the Sauna, I had not seen Franz leave, but only heard the door opened and closed. I had not heard it locked. I had noticed the door when we entered. I had noticed everything. It had a proper lock, that door; it was not a Yale or Ingersoll or any Swiss equivalent. The key would still be on the inside; Franz would have expected the others to lock the door after him, and they had not done so, allowing me a chance of escape. It would be escape naked, and at a time when there would be nobody about, no journalist or accredited person, to accost for help, only the Night Porter who, as I had already been told, would swear that I had not returned, but yet might not be prepared to become a direct accessory to murder. If I could find a way to reach that door I must do so, and before Franz returned.

Tock! There was an electric clock on the wall. The minute-hand moved fowards at the end of each minute, and made a small sound. Four twenty-five! That was another consideration in my favour; it was just as well that I had taken my time in making our escape from the house on the mountain, flailing about with the lid of a thunderbox instead of examining the hinges of the windows. Hotels come awake early. By six, the staff would be stirring. They might not be stirring here, down in the Sauna, but their presence elsewhere would inhibit the job of clearing up and moving my body. Even down here . . . why not? There are people who enjoy an early-morning plunge; one never meets them, but one knows they exist. I allowed myself to imagine the Egyptian rattling the door-handle. The telephone rang again, just three times, and stopped.

Jerry and the young priest were by now thoroughly unsettled. They stared at the telephone and at each other. They were most unlikely now to remember to lock the door. The young priest took out his Swiss Army knife, opened it, closed it again, and put it back in his pocket. I decided to add to their unsettlement if I could. 'Sounds like a signal.'

'It was not a signal,' the young priest said. 'It could not have been a signal. We do not expect a signal. It would have no meaning.'

'Could have been a signal for me.'

'We should kill him now, and go.'

'Don't be stupid, Dieter.' Jerry came and sat miserably by my flank on the marble slab. 'Look,' he said, 'put it this way. You don't want anything to happen to Pru.'

'Do you?'

'Of course I bloody don't. She's half my living. I'm talking economics here.'

'Look at the time. You'd better let me go. I keep telling you I don't know anything, and by the time you've made sure of that, it'll be daylight outside and a vacuum cleaner going full blast in every corridor.' I sat up on the slab, and the young priest pushed me down again roughly. Too early, but it had added to the unease. *Tock!* I did not know what to make of the telephone; that second call had sounded intentional.

'We have to wait for Franz.'

'And if he says you're to kill Pru? Rape her and then murder her? Quickly because there's hardly any time? Will you do it?'

Jerry's eyes swivelled sideways. The young priest's hand had gone to his pocket again.

I said to Jerry, '*You're* not armed, I suppose?'

'No.'

'Jerry, explain your position please 'to Mr Hatcher.'

Jerry said to me, 'Don't push it, Paul. If Franz gets instructions to kill her, there's nothing I can do to save her. Or you.' He stood up, and moved away, the young priest watching him. 'Just co-operate. That way we'll all stay alive.'

'I am co-operating. I don't know anything. I can't tell you any more that that.' If the young priest was going to watch Jerry instead of me, that was already a turn for the better. I sat up again, and this time was not pushed back.

Tock! Jerry said, 'He's taking his time.'

'Does he have far to go?'

'There's a pay-phone in Reception.'

'Mr Hatcher does not need this information, Jerry.'

146

'What information? He knows there's a pay-phone in Reception. It's hardly a secret, for Christ's sake.' *Tock!*

I said, 'It seems odd that he couldn't have phoned from here. But I suppose he didn't want you listening to what he had to say about Pru.' I stood up. 'He's certainly been gone a long time.'

'There could have been someone in the phone-box already?'

'At twenty to five? Well, I did warn you there'd be people about.'

Jerry said to the young priest, 'This is going wrong!'

The young priest said to me, 'Keep away from that door.' *Tock!* He could see the door from where he was standing, and now noticed what I, finding it hard to believe, had noticed already. 'Where's the key?' He turned towards me. 'You! Where's the key?' His eyes looked very odd behind his spectacles, and I became worried about the Swiss Army knife. I did not wish him to be unsettled to the point of going out of control.

I extended my hands to him, palms upwards. 'I'm naked,' I said. 'No hiding place. Anyway you know bloody well I haven't been anywhere near that door. Why couldn't Franz have taken the key?'

Jerry said, 'Right! He took the key with him, and locked the door from the outside.'

'Locked us in. The young priest was sweating copiously, and his eyes were rolling—did I imagine a fleck of foam at his lips? He looked like a mad horse. In spite of his readiness to flourish the Swiss Army knife, I guessed that he was no more used to situations of this sort than I was myself.

'Why not? Relax, Dieter! He'll be back.' *Tock!*

I said, 'Of course, if anything should have happened to him—'

'Be quiet!'

'—any delay, phone out of order, heart attack, street accident, anything like that; it would be a bit embarrassing.' *Tock!* You will find it hard to believe that I was beginning to

147

enjoy myself. Perhaps only the memory of it is enjoyable. If Franz had returned at that moment, it would not have been enjoyable. As matters were, I had begun to feel in control of the situation, if only for a while. I walked forward, still naked, to get a better view of the door. I knew, as they did not, that Franz had not locked it behind him. It seemed to me unlikely therefore that he had taken the key. If he had not taken the key, someone else had. The logic of it clicked over as smoothly in my mind as beads on an abacus. It is usually only in daydreams that one reasons with such clarity.

Jerry said, 'Give him another five minutes, then we'll decide what to do. We don't have to stay locked in here; we can phone the Night Porter.'

It was a situation much to be desired if they did. I decided to push Jerry further. 'I suppose if Franz has been given his instructions, he might have gone straight up to Pru's room. Spare your feelings. He could hardly rely on you to help.'

'Oh, yes!' My explanation had calmed the young priest a little, but it had, as I had intended, the opposite effect on Jerry, who went swiftly to the door, turned the handle, and pulled. The door opened smoothly, and Franz's body fell into the room. A falling body will take up curious attitudes when it hits the floor, but it seemed to me that, even so, the neck was oddly twisted.

In order to close the door again, Jerry would have had to move the body's legs. He seemed reluctant to do so. In the pantry, the espresso machine was boiling over. *Tock!* The young priest crouched by Franz's head, put his own hands between his knees, and began to rock backwards and forwards, weeping. Jerry said to me, 'Get dressed.'

'Dead?'

'Get *dressed*!' The young priest rocked and wept, his sobs broken by words of German. I guessed that he and Franz had been lovers, but could not feel sorry. Jerry said to him, 'And you! On your feet! We're getting out of here.'

I dressed as quickly as I could. 'Why not leave me? I'll only be in your way. It's clear you've got enemies.'

Jerry said to the young priest, 'Keep him quiet. Kill him if he tries to run. There's a way out through the basement.' The young priest nodded, calmed by the orders and by the fact that someone else had taken charge, and began to remove the gold chain from Franz's neck, the gold bracelet from one wrist and the gold watch from the other, and the signet-ring of platinum and amethyst from his finger. I do not think he was robbing the body, but reclaiming love-tokens.

I started to ask where they planned to take me, but the young priest hit me across the mouth with a hand full of jewellery, and split my lip. *Tock!* Twelve minutes to five. Would it be daylight yet in Liechtenstein on March 28th, and did the way out through the basement lead to the front of the hotel or somewhere more private?

I walked in single file between Jerry and the young priest, and wondered towards what part of my back the knife might be pointing. We emerged into an area of lawn and shrubs and into darkness.

I tensed my muscles. It was time to leap into that darkness, dive behind shrubs, run and dodge, make my escape before I could be bundled into a car and driven back up the mountain. I must do it, and at once. Or maybe later. Maybe there would be a better time, halfway to the car-park, or in the car-park itself where the ground would be harder, and perhaps there would be lights. If I were to try to make my escape now, the young priest would be expecting it. I imagined the sharpened Swiss Army knife curving upwards into flesh, stripping away fat, grating against bone. They would leave me lying among the shrubs, hideously, mortally wounded, liver, kidneys, bowels all cut about and bleeding, vomit-stained and in pain, and any early-riser, looking down from a window, would think me drunk, and draw the curtains.

When I was a child we had a cat called Bandy. The fiction was that he was my cat; I fed him; it was thought that, by looking after pets, children learned to consider the welfare of others. Of course he roamed, as all tom cats do. One

149

evening in winter, with homework to be done and Bandy late for his supper, I heard him mewing outside the back door, went to let him in, found him crouching there, picked him up, then threw him down again, swearing at him, because he had been sick all down his front, and my sweater was stained with it. In fact he had not been sick, but in a fight. His stomach had been ripped open; it had been Bandy's guts, spilling out of his stomach, which had stained my sweater. He was taken to the vet, and put down. He had come home for help, and I had thrown him down, dying as he was, and sworn at him.

Jerry said, 'Don't try anything, Paul.' He had fallen back beside me, and took my arm in his. 'We'll just walk round to the car-park in a friendly way.'

A voice which I recognized as that of the man in the brown suit said, 'Stay where you are.' It was a quiet, but commanding voice. I felt Jerry's arm go rigid in mine. 'Might as well put your hands up while you're at it. Over your heads.' I raised my hands above my head, but felt the knife touch my side. A beam of what must have been the light from a powerful torch illuminated our heads, and then went out. 'Both hands, if you don't mind, unless you want a bullet in your back.' The knife left my side, and the young priest raised his hand. The torch was switched on again. 'Now drop the knife.' I heard the knife hit the grass, and the light went out. 'Any other weapons, Mr Hatcher, as far as you know?'

'Not as far as I know.'

'Now, on the command "One", Mr Hatcher will take four paces backwards, doing the best not to bump into any of the herbage. One!' I took four careful steps backwards. The beam of the torch shone out again, on and off. Jerry and the young priest still had their hands in the air. 'Good! Break away now if you wish, Mr Hatcher, but stay close to me. Just take care not to get between my pistol and these gentlemen.'

I could see him now against the wall of the hotel. He was alone. He held the torch in his left hand, and in his right something which I supposed to be a pistol with a silencer. I assumed that he would wish me to help him conduct Jerry and the young priest to the local police-station.

'Do you want me to tie their hands?' I had no rope, but it could be found. The hotel would have some.

'No, I don't think so.'

'What are you going to do with them?'

'Let them go. They're only small fry. You hear that, you two? You're to be let go.'

'But they're murderers. They would have murdered me. That interior decorator, you told me yourself—'

'No evidence. Isn't that right, Mr Graves?' The torch was flicked on and off like the beam of a light-house, but irregularly.

Jerry said, 'Nothing to do with me.'

'Exactly!'

'Alright. *I'll* make a complaint.'

'You don't want to involve the local police, Mr Hatcher. What would you complain about? A little horseplay? Practical jokes in a Sauna between gentlemen? Then there's the matter of Franz. (You'd better get that seen to, you two. Report it, and get him tidied away.) We're all murderers in this game, Mr Hatcher. The only difference is, I work for a nationalised industry, and these two are in the private sector.'

The young priest said, 'It was you who killed my friend?'

'Unfortunate necessity.'

'With piano wire?'

'Silk rope, since you ask. I prefer that. You run a risk with piano wire; the head's liable to come off altogether, which leads to mess just where you don't want it. The thugs, you know, back in India—thuggee; they used silk cords. Knew what they were about. You can learn from history.' I noticed that, as well as the business with the torch, he kept moving his position slightly. 'Now, on the command "One", you two will take a couple of paces forward, away from that knife, and stand by for further

151

orders. Two paces, then stop, hands still in the air. One!'
The torch light came on.

I had noticed in Pru's bedroom a bedside lamp, with a
shade of watered silk and a heavy ceramic base. That lamp,
or one like it, now came crashing down from above onto the
left shoulder of the man in the brown suit, knocking him
over. As he fell, the torch dropped from his hand, and
remained lit, but illuminating only the patch of lawn in front
of it. I jumped away into the darkness, and remained poised
for flight. Jerry stopped where he was. The young priest
stooped for the knife, then launched himself towards the
man in the brown suit, who was getting hastily to his feet,
and knocked him over again. My eyes had adjusted to the
darkness, and I could see the blade of the knife, which the
young priest held in front of him, so that the whole weight
of his body was behind it. The gun went off, making a noise
like a potato-pistol. The young priest howled.

The man in the brown suit picked up the torch, and stood
up. The torch illuminated the young priest, who lay on the
ground, whimpering with pain. 'Don't make such a fuss,
lad.' The man in the brown suit sounded breathless. 'It's
only your knee-cap. If you lived in Ulster, you'd be well
used to that.' I could hear that there was an element of self-
control in his voice. He was hurt, I was sure of it, but they
must not know they had wounded him.

The young priest took no notice of the comforting words
of the man in the brown suit, but continued to whimper. The
man said to Jerry, 'Keep the stupid bastard quiet, and get
him out of here, unless you want to wake the hotel.' The
young priest stopped whimpering, and Jerry came cau-
tiously into the illuminated area, and helped him to his feet.
The man said, 'I don't suppose that lady of yours would
have been so free with the bedside lamp if she'd known
what was due to happen to her. Now on your way, and don't
forget; I want that body cleared up before anyone trips over
it.'

The young priest leaned on Jerry's shoulder, Jerry

covered his mouth with one hand in case the pain of dragging his wounded leg across grass should cause him to cry out again, and the two of them moved away, held in the beam of the torch until it lost its power. I said quietly, 'You're hurt, aren't you? Is it bad?'

'Bad enough to need seeing to. Help me round to the front. I could do with a Jimmy Riddle, but we haven't the time.'

We could hear a car leave the park, and it passed the front of the hotel as we turned the corner. Jerry was driving; he looked sideways anxiously, but did not see us. I supposed that he would deliver the young priest to somewhere in the town, make his report, and then return to the hotel, perhaps to assist the Night Porter and other confederates to dispose of Franz. Would Franz turn up later in the restaurant as Game Pie, and would Clinton Bard send him back? The man in the brown suit was giving me more of his weight now; I began to be afraid of letting him fall. He said, 'You won't have any more trouble with that lot now they know we're onto them.'

'What am I to do?'

'Stay. You're on the Jury. You've got a job to do. Five thousand francs in it, isn't there?'

An old-fashioned motor-bike with a sidecar was parked a little way down the road. One of the press photographers seemed to be in charge of it; none of those photographers looked more than sixteen years old. He saw us, came running up the road, and helped me support my burden for the rest of the way.

I said, 'Careful! He's hurt.'

'He can bloody see that.' The man in the brown suit spoke to the boy in German. The boy nodded, and opened the door of the sidecar.

The man in the brown suit said, 'Look! Something to tell you. Not pleasant. Don't want you to read it in the papers.'

'Yes?' I thought immediately of Bonzo. Had they found her? Was she hurt? But nothing that happened to Bonzo would make the newspapers. Had the *Radical* finally ceased publication, then, and left me jobless? The man in the brown suit held on to the frame of the sidecar, his wound clearly needing attention, yet reluctant to go without telling me something he was reluctant to say.

'They got to your wife.'

'Who did?'

'Not this lot. Bloody Yanks! Over-enthusiastic! No finesse, you see. Bungle everything they touch, in my opinion. Arseholes!'

I said, 'You're not a plain-clothes policeman, then?'

'Same line of country.'

'What happened?'

'Interrogation.'

'And?'

'Usual thing. Went too far. Had to cover up.'

'Are you trying to tell me that American agents—what did they do? You're not trying to tell me . . . ?' One makes these noises. I knew that he was trying to tell me that American agents had killed my wife. It was all the same thing; he had said so himself. Some were in the private and some in the public sector, but they behaved in much the same way.

'Messy business. Had to cover themselves, you see. Thought so anyway. Sorry.' He lowered himself carefully into the sidecar. 'Couldn't keep them out, not with two of their own people involved. I can't bear a heavy hand.' The photographer kicked his motorcycle into life. The engine roared, and the sidecar shook violently. 'Oh shit! Bloody hurts,' said the man in the brown suit, and was driven away.

They had killed Anne, and 'they' were not the people who had beaten the interior decorator to death and would have done the same to me in the Sauna, nor (I supposed) the fake-policemen who had murdered Gavin's grandmother, but American agents, the C.I.A. or some such, a group of whose involvement I had known nothing whatever, over-enthusiastic counterparts of the man in the brown suit, who could not be kept out because 'two of their own people' were involved, by which he must have meant the presidential aide and the N.A.T.O. general. These people were not attempting, as the man in the brown suit had done, to discover the identities of those who had set up the murder of the boy. Their concern was only to suppress the evidence. I imagined that the man in the brown suit and his colleagues would be concerned to suppress the evidence also, but at least he had been around to protect me. There had been nobody around to protect Anne.

I found myself consumed with helpless rage. I raged against myself. Oh, no doubt she had said or done something to draw attention to herself, but she could not have done so if I had never confided in her to begin with. I should have known, did know, that she was an investigative journalist down to her bones; she could not deny that instinct. She had known that I had the negatives, and they would have had that knowledge out of her. (Was that why the man in the brown suit had said 'two of their own people involved'? Unless I already knew about the negatives, the phrase would have been meaningless to me.) She had not known where they were, or thought she did not, because I had told her that I was removing them from Bonzo's collar. My flat would have been turned upside down by now, upholstery slit, the books torn to pieces; they would use no finesse there either. Even if they were finally to go after Bonzo also, Anne had not known where I had taken her. A Kennels—a great many Kennels are advertised in *Our Dogs*, and in any case I had not, in the end, gone to a Kennels at all.

They did not know where Bonzo was, but no doubt, given time, they could find out. 'Stay. You're on the Jury. You've got a job to do.' It would suit them all if I were to remain in Vaduz, well out of the way. Nobody now of the public-sector murderers wanted to hurt me; they would far rather get what they wanted without having to go to such extremes. As for the private sector, the man in the brown suit would have been right about them. Their aim had been to prevent the security services from finding a link between the negatives and themselves, and now they had failed;

through me the link had been discovered. By patient enquiry, working back from whatever organisation had subsidised the Festival and made it a condition that I should be on the Jury, through however extended a series of holding companies and nominees, the identity (or at least, if he were resident in Eastern Europe the geographical location) of the rich and powerful corrupter could be discovered; it would be mainly paperwork now. The senior operatives of his organisation would be scattering; I was no longer important to them for any purpose.

I was safe at Vaduz, safe from both the private sector and the public sector, with only a little embarrassment to discomfort me, at meeting Pru again. But I was angry; I no longer wished to be safe. Oh, I had no doubt that the participants in that original murder would be punished in some way, discreetly, and eased out of their public positions. I had no doubt either that the publication of those photographs could do nothing but harm internationally to my own country and the N.A.T.O. Alliance. But the security agencies had gone too far; 'over-enthusiastically' they had killed my wife, and as for the murder of the old lady, whatever group, public or private, had been responsible, it had been an official cover-up. I wanted to blow that whole cover-up wide open, even if, in my attempt to do so, I should attract the attention of the American arseholes.

There was a chance that nobody would be watching me, since the man in the brown suit was temporarily out of action, and had no reason to believe that I would not stay. They would not have told me about my wife's death at all, except that I would have read it in the papers, which are on sale in Europe a day late; therefore they already knew that an account of some sort had appeared in Sunday's papers for me to read that Monday morning. They knew that I should not believe what I read, and had wished me to know that they were not responsible. The man in the brown suit, who had appeared to be so anxious to prepare me and spare my feelings, had actually only been saying, 'It wasn't us.'

I began to pack, then changed my mind. I walked out of

the hotel in overcoat and muffler as if for an early-morning stroll, my wallet and passport in an inside pocket. The suitcase would have been too heavy to carry, and would have attracted attention in Reception. Leaving it in my room would suggest that I was still in residence, so that my absence might not be noticed until it was time to leave for the cinema.

There is no railway in Liechtenstein. I went to the Bus Station, and asked a girl waiting for the early-morning bus how to get to Zurich. She spoke English. I was to take the bus to Sargans, and an Inter-City train thereafter. It was easy. I was at the Airport in just over two hours. I used my Access card to book myself on the next scheduled flight to London. If one has become accustomed to the probability of being murdered, one ceases to worry about the payment of a monthly credit account.

It was eight thirty on the Monday morning—seven thirty in London because of the time difference. I bought myself the Sunday papers from a shop in the Airport Concourse. The story was on the front page of all three of the quality Sundays. There had been two deaths, that of my wife and a young northern photographer, with whom, it was suggested, she had been having some kind of sado-masochistic fling at her flat. She had been found tied up, her naked body covered with cigarette burns, her tights stuffed into her mouth, and he, in remorse, had hanged himself with his own long johns. My wife was not a masochist, far from it, nor did I believe that any ambitious mulberry-eyed young northerner on his first date with a celebrity would have worn long johns. I would never have been likely to accept such a story, but without evidence would seem only paranoid if I were to accuse operatives of the C.I.A. of the murder.

On the plane I discovered that I was hungry as well as angry, and asked for a second breakfast, offering to pay for it, but there was no provision for that, and I was refused. It was also taken amiss that, on hearing a routine flight-announcement that Paris was below and on our right, though obscured by cloud, I burst into tears, and continued to blub for the rest of the journey. Nothing was said, but the lady next to me moved her seat. It would have taken so little physical persuasion by Franz and his friends to have made me tell everything, but my wife had endured pain longer, and had forced the American arseholes to go too far.

We had a son, Anne and I, but he was born with spina bifida, the lesion being high up the back, and the surgeon advised us that it would be better for everyone to let Nature take its course. It had been a prolonged and difficult birth. I had been by her side for much of the time, smelled her sweat, watched her endure the pain which she was unwilling to express, even after they had told her to do so. 'Scream if you like, dear,' the midwife had said. 'We're used to it. Scream and pant.' Anne had shaken her head angrily. She would pant, but she would not scream. I held her hand for as long as I was allowed, and she squeezed my fingers as she pushed, but at the end they sent me away, and I did not see the actual birth. The lesion was much too high for remedial surgery to have done much good. The quality of the child's life, the surgeon said, would be inferior.

THE WRONG MAN

AT HEATHROW I USED MY CREDIT CARD AGAIN TO HIRE A car, and drove north and west, through Berkshire and Oxfordshire and on into Warwickshire, to recover the negatives and Bonzo, my dog. At first I took the two motorways, M4 and M40, and then, just before Oxford, switched to minor roads, and I do not believe that I was followed. I stopped at Islip, as if to look in the windows of an Antique Shop, and then again at Cropredy to buy orange juice, marked those cars which went past me, and looked again for them thereafter, but did not find them. There was no car near me at Mollington, and none behind me when I took the turn to Davey's cottage.

There was no reason for anyone to follow me, because no reason why anyone should know I had returned. I would not have been missed until ten thirty Vaduz time (nine thirty English), and then only by the Festival people. Who would tell the man in the brown suit?—certainly not Jerry. If the boy with the motorbike who had driven him away were really a press photographer, and not merely posing as one, then he might get the news, but not for some time, and there was no reason why he should guess immediately that I had returned to London; he would be more likely to suspect that Jerry's employers had, after all, decided to do away with me, and would be momentarily vexed at his misjudgement. Nobody would check the passenger-list of my flight until long after it had landed, or the records of the car-hire firms until after it was clear that I had not returned to South Kensington, or to my wife's flat, or the offices of the

Radical. Provided that, once I had arrived at Davey's cottage, I did not use the hired car again, I could roam freely.

Nobody was in when I arrived, so I waited in the car. After a while, the four of them returned across fields, the two Jack Russells on a lead because of sheep, and Bonzo loping free. If my son had been born without a disability, and had lived, I could not have continued as a reviewer of films: I should have had to have found another job, better paid.

I got out of the car as they approached, and stood waiting. She did not run to meet me, made none of those whining yelping reproachful noises with which she had been accustomed to greet my return to the flat, but while Davey was closing the gate of the field behind him, she walked up to me, licked my hand, and remained by me. The Jack Russells ignored me. Davey said, 'Did they cancel your Festival? You won't get a refund of her board-money, I'm afraid.' He walked over, and took a closer look at me. I had washed the cut on my lip in my room at the Statler, but had been unable to find an adhesive dressing, and it had begun bleeding again in the bus, so that a scab of dried blood had formed on it. Also there were bruises on my throat where Franz had been applying pressure on the glands. 'Been in a fight?'

'You couldn't call it a fight.'

'Come inside, and I'll clean you up.'

'I'm rather hungry.'

'Missed your breakfast?'

'They don't give you much on the plane.' Dinner with Pru at Vaduz, which, even allowing for the time-difference, was only just over fifteen hours away, seemed to have happened during another existence. Loss of appetite is a more usual reaction than hunger to stress, but I had missed a night's sleep, during which my body had expended a great deal of energy. Alternatively one might suggest that I was frightened and insecure, that the underpinnings of my usual way of life had all been knocked away, and that I needed the symbolic reassurance of being given food. Take your pick of the reasons, emotional or physical; I had been refused a second breakfast on the plane, and was still hungry.

You will have realised that, although I knew I was going to do something, and that I was going to do it at once, I still did not know what I was going to do. Working through my own pupils and the storyboard in order to gain access to the photographic facilities of the East Hounslow College would take too long. Much of my time on the plane had been spent in tears, the rest in daydreaming. I had acted out in my imagination the interview in which I denounced the C.I.A. for my wife's murder, and produced the negatives in evidence, but I knew well enough that I should never get that far, and even if I did it, it would never be transmitted. Nothing is live, you see, not nowadays, nothing but sport. Interviews, news-footage, they are all, as my wife's own programme was, recorded and edited, just as the newspapers have to be printed before they are published, so that there is always time for the colleagues of the man in the brown suit to censor them in the national interest. If I were to try to give an interview, nothing would come of it except that the negatives, my only evidence, would be confiscated.

It came to me, as Davey dabbed at my lip with the cotton wool soaked in a warm solution of bicarbonate of soda, that even if I were to follow my orginal plan, and sent prints to every newspaper, publication could still be prevented.

Davey's touch was gentle, his eyes concerned. He said, 'You never told me how you came by Bonzo.'

Everything now was to be told. I told him everything. I ate quantities of wholemeal bread and butter, spring lettuce and Cotswold cheese, drank a pot of tea, talked and talked while Davey listened, asking very few questions and those only, it seemed to me, to indicate that he understood; they were not questioning questions. I told him of Gavin's death and my wife's death, and all that had happened in between, and felt that, just as my hunger was abated by the food, so too my helpless anger was dissipated by by the act of telling, of sharing so much that I had kept to myself, and the sensation of tears behind the eyes always ready to spill uselessly out, which I realised had been with me for weeks, now disappeared, and there remained only a simple solution to get the secret out and the business over.

At the end he said, 'You'll be wanting to use the Dark Room, I expect,' and I realised who Gavin's collaborator had been.

I said, 'I'd never have thought of you as a blackmailer.'

'I told you I'd do anything for money.'

'Unless it was against your principles.'

'Where Gavin was concerned, my principles were flexible.'

He stared at me, daring me to disapprove. I said, 'He must have caused you considerable grief.'

'Yes. Not least by dying.'

I should have known. Bonzo was never Gavin's dog, had shown no real attachment to him, forsook him in danger. She had been given to him, complete with pedigree, to protect him perhaps (though she had not done so) or to give him at least a feeling of protection, to be a part of Davey, unnoticed but always with him. She was a man's dog. Had she been turned off by the female disguise, confused by it, and found reassurance in me? I said, 'It must have given you rather a shock when I showed up here with her.'

'Oh, you were obviously harmless. She wouldn't have taken to you otherwise.'

After lunch we removed Bonzo's collar, unpicked the protective camouflage, took out the negatives, and proceeded to Davey's Dark Room, which was an extension of the Tool Shed. Bonzo waited outside the door for us. She was like a woman with two lovers, showing favour to both, preference to neither.

The prints Davey made were clear in detail, most unlike my own fuzzy grey attempts at enlargements by means of the slide-projector. He made two sets and, when they were dry, gave one to me, examining the other critically and unemotionally. 'Not bad.' I supposed that he must have seen them before, having made a set for Gavin to send to the

162

minister. I myself still found it painful to look at them. One could see clearly now that the four naked men were in a Sauna, not the bath itself but the area outside. The boy was lying face downwards on a marble slab, his head supported by one of those wooden blocks used by masseurs, which are shaped like the bottom part of a guillotine. It was not, of course, the Sauna of the Statler Hotel; the four men could never have been brought together in Vaduz without attracting notice. It would be located in some private house. To own one's own Sauna must be common practice among the rich; one sees advertisements for them in the glossy magazines, and even I was once a guest in one belonging to an architect, friend of my wife, who had set it up in a wood in Wiltshire. The architect's Sauna was more spartanly appointed than this, and certainly had no marble slab for massage. This would have been the private toy of some very rich person, with facilities for taking photographs of its users which would have been even more private, and not a toy.

Davey said, 'You don't care now if people know that you sent the pictures?'

'No.'

'You just want to be sure they're published?'

'Yes.'

'Anyway, once they've been published, you're safe. Secret's out. Killing you then would only be counter-productive.'

'Right.'

'Didn't you tell me you work for a magazine?'

The idea was immediately seductive. Instead of possibly faked, probably crank photographs, arriving anonymously at the offices of all the news-media like bait indiscriminately scattered, I could publish in the *Radical*, and keep control. The news-media would have to check on the photographs, allowing the colleagues of the man in the brown suit to slap on D-Notices, or whatever it is they do nowadays in our democracy to keep important information from the voters, but for the *Radical* I myself, an experienced and trusted

163

member of staff, would be a witness to their authenticity; I would write copy to go with them, explaining how they came into my possession. It would be the scoop of the century, and might, if I could persuade my editor to increase the print-run, quadruple our circulation, an increase which it would take us at least a year to lose again. I said, 'I can't go back there. By now they'll be looking for me.'

'Where's your mag printed?'

'Northampton.'

'Well, then? I'll take these prints into blocks, and you can take copy along with you, make up a new page, and substitute it.'

'It doesn't work like that nowadays.'

When, as an undergraduate, I had been Film Editor of *The Isis*, the magazine had been printed by a method called 'flatbed'. Lead type had been set in em widths and combined in a forme with blocks of the art-work to make a page, and the pages had been printed four at a time, very much on the principle of a child's Printing Set, by pressing the inked forme onto blank paper. When I first joined the *Radical*, it was printed on the same principle (not that we ever used photographs), and so were its competitors, and all small-circulation magazines, and books. In the old days, the Assistant Editor would spend the whole of every Wednesday at the printers, supervising the final make-up of the pages, making last-minute corrections and additions. It would certainly have been possible then to substitute a page.

It has all changed now. Even the *Radical* is printed by photo-litho, the editorial galleys produced by what seems to be a kind of word-processor, and, after correction, combined with the advertising, and pasted together to make a page which will then be photographed. Squadrons of lead type are no longer moved about with tweezers; instead strips of paper are cut to shape with a razor and pasted on top of other pieces. So far the process has been a back-and-forth business between the *Radical* office and Messrs Photophrase, only five streets away, which performs the same service for five other national magazines, to wit *Combo!*,

Home-Computing Weekly, Video-Grid, New Sociology and *The Alternative Bioptic Advertiser.* What next happens is that the photographed pages of the issue, looking like pieces of brown celluloid, are sent by despatch-rider to Northampton, there to be transferred to thin aluminium sheets, which are fitted onto a roller, which prints the paper by the rotary process. And these Northampton printers also print other weekly national magazines, though not the same ones. The old personal relationship of the editorial staff with the printers in the days of heavy-metal and flat-bed printing, compounded of surliness on one side at the prospect of having to move the type about after it had already been made up into the forme, and a sycophantic anxiety on the other, no longer exists. Making corrections is no trouble to the new breed of photo-printers, who smile perpetually and sometimes offer to share their lunch-time sandwiches, and Heavy Metal now is a kind of Rock music.

I explained most of this to Davey, whose forays into the world of what is called 'commercial art' had taken him no further than the offices of the Art Directors of advertising agencies. I said 'It's such a small staff at the *Radical* that even I've been to Photophrase sometimes, just to help out when the Assistant Editor's been sick or on holiday; they pay me *per diem.* But nobody ever goes to Northampton. There'd be no point, with the page already photographed.'

'What happens at Northampton? Exactly.'

'I told you. They print the run. Twelve thousand copies.'

'What happens to the twelve thousand?'

'Some come back to the office, to be sent out individually to subscribers; that's just under a thousand. About half of those go abroad, mostly to British Council Reading Rooms.'

'And the other eleven thousand?'

'Distributed to newsagents.'

'By whom?'

'I don't know. A distributor, I suppose.'

'From where? London or Northampton?'

'I don't know that either.'

'You don't know much,' said Davey. 'Have you got anything to identify you as a member of staff?''

'Contributor. There's my Press Card.'

'Should do.'

'It's in the flat.'

'Alright. I'll forge you a letter from the editor. Is it still Harvey Thing?'

'It ceased to be Harvey Thing fifteen years ago.'

'The Advertising Manager might be better. I suppose you don't know his name?'

'You've got a plan, haven't you?'

'I always have a plan,' said Davey.

It was a simple plan but, as it seemed to both of us, a good one. There would be no persuading my editor to increase the *Radical's* print-run, no advance discussion at all except between Davey and myself; nobody else would know what we were about. There was much work to be done on what remained of that day and the next two. On the Thursday, since the cross-country train service is very poor, Davey would take me in the sidecar of his motor-cycle to Northampton, and leave me at the Railway Station, where I could easily find a taxi to take me to the printers, carrying with me a suitcase which would contain what we had spent two days in preparing. Since I could not insert a page, or in any way tamper with pages already photographed, I should be inserting additional advertising matter. Such a thing is often done, though more usually with local papers, when a leaflet advertising the week's Special Offers at Safeways, Tesco or Fine Fare is tucked between the pages of one's *Guardian* or *Courier*. We would use a single sheet, folded over and sealed on the other three sides, the outside bearing only the words, 'OPEN HERE TO FIND OUT IF YOU HAVE WON A PRIZE.' Again, the device is familiar: The *Reader's Digest*, The Automobile Association and the makers of thermal underwear all use a similar form of promotion in their direct-mail advertising. We should be combining two already familiar advertising practices, and I, known already as a regular contributor to the *Radical* over many years, and bearing a letter from the Advertising Manager, should arouse no suspicion among the printers.

The scheme had an additional advantage. Since the inserts were already sealed, the printers themselves would not know what was being sent out. Nobody would know before those rational and fair-minded persons, the opinion leaders, the upper-middle-brow élite, the readers of the *Radical*, who would buy the issue at newsagents all over the country, or receive it with the rest of the morning's post (*Mind*, The Anti-Apartheid League, the Goethe Institute), scoff a little at the inclusion of such an insertion, open it to know whether they had won a prize, and find that all of them had done so (which is again not unusual), and that the prize consisted of a page of six photographs and three hundred words of copy, now beyond suppression.

Davey was a little disappointed at not being able to use his own hand-made paper with flecks on it, but photographs could not be reproduced on such a surface. However, his hand-press was used for more than his own poetry: he had other paper in stock. We could choose between the card from which he made picture postcards of local views, photographed by himself, and the glossy paper used for a steady summer-seller, *Antiquities of the Edge Hills*, with a special section devoted to the probable sites of the Red Horse of Tysoe Vale (now lost), as revealed by aerial reconnaissance. In the end, in order to make up our twelve thousand, we had to use both. The suitcase was heavy.

On that Monday afternoon, March 26th, Davey prepared the blocks, and I slept on his bed, with Bonzo at my feet. He woke me for an evening meal. We talked, listened to music, watched television on a black-and-white set which had ghosts on most channels. Then I slept again, this time on a camp-bed in the living-room, comforted by the glow of the dying fire; Bonzo, unable to find room on my legs, padded between me and the Jack Russells in the kitchen, grumbling. I woke early with the daylight, the words of the text which I must write to accompany the photographs already forming in my head, and got out of bed to write them down. For the rest of Tuesday and Wednesday, Davey and I worked the hand-press together, a monotonous but satisfying operation. I was happy, working with a friend towards the achievement of a dangerous, but necesssary, object. The ghosts were confined to the television; we never mentioned Gavin.

On the Thursday morning, I telephoned the printers, as if from the *Radical* office, warning them to expect me. There was no need to reach Northampton early. The insertion of the extra material could not be made until the copies were already stapled, and that would not be until the afternoon. I would do the job myself, if union rules permitted, and if not, an authorised union member would do it, and I should be by his side. I did not know whether the copies would be returned to London by van or train, but in any case I could beg a ride, with my by then empty suitcase, back to the Railway Station. The van-driver would believe I was returning to London. In fact, I should go by train to Leamington, via Coventry, phoning Davey to let him know when to meet me. On the Friday, Bonzo and I would return to South Kensington in the hired car. It would not matter then that the security services of two countries would know where to find me. The secret would already be out. Even American arseholes would not kill for revenge, and if they did I could not help it.

The simple plan was simply executed. The insertions were made by an apprentice with pink hair, under my own supervision, so that I was able to ensure that none of them was opened. Nobody bothered us, and it all went without incident until almost the end of the operation, when the foreman picked up a copy containing the inserted sheet to take home.

I had forgotten. Lead-type or photo-litho, it makes no difference; the foreman of a printing firm would be a thinking man, a reading man, and the least of his perks would be a copy to take home. He would sit in his usual armchair, in front of the fire, and dip into the magazine before he had his tea. 'OPEN HERE TO FIND OUT IF

YOU HAVE WON A PRIZE'; the formula succeeds; one may not return the 'YES' envelope, but one takes that first step. The foreman was a thinking man, accustomed to print, to weekly journalism if not daily; he would be on the phone within minutes to *The Daily Express*. The secret would be out too soon, and there would be time to suppress it.

Did I think these thoughts in sequence, or did I merely react instinctively to any divergence from the plan as a threat, which must be countered? Only a small pile of undoctored copies remained. I took one, and offered it. 'Have one of these. Save Gary the bother. His fingers are flagging.' The apprentice gave the sideways grin of one whose fingers never flagged. 'It's only advertising,' I said.

The foreman hesitated. 'But if there's a prize.'

He played Haydn quartets on Friday nights with three friends. He was a man I could reach; I was sure of it. 'When there's a prize for everyone, Alastair, you know what sort of bloody price it is. Free condensed books would be my guess.'

The foreman put his doctored copy back on the pile, and accepted instead the copy I gave him. He walked off before we had finished, to watch the copies being tied into bundles, ready for the van, which was just as well, since, when all the copies contained inserts, there was now one insert over.

The apprentice looked at it and at me. 'Prize, is it?'

'Not worth having.'

He picked up the sealed and folded page, which was one of those for which we had used the heavy post-card paper, on which the seal had been less effective. He picked at the corner with his thumb-nail. 'Might as well take a look.'

What do they think of, the teenagers of his generation? I have no contact of any kind with them, neither emotional nor intellectual. I had met Alastair, the foreman, for the first time that day, and we had spoken immediately as equals, so that I had been able to deceive him as easily as one deceives a friend. I could not deceive Gary, who knew that something was up.

I took out my wallet, as Gary pushed back a little more of

the corner of the folded sheet. I said, 'A boy of your age needs money more than condensed books.' There was a pause as Gary gave himself to thought. Then he said, 'It'll cost you.' I handed over a ten-pound note, and received in return the folded sheet, which I put into my pocket For some reason, Gary's cheeks had taken on the same color as his hair.

I suppose I may have saved both their lives.

Back at Davey's cottage, I lay awake for much of that night. I knew that I must do what is called 'the decent thing', but not whether I had the decency to do it.

Bonzo was not mine, by right of gift or purchase. She belonged to Davey, was happy in his company, and happy in the country. Take what walks one may, around squares, down streets, through Kensington Gardens, a third-floor flat in the Royal Borough will never be a proper place for an alsatian. If I wanted a dog, there were dogs more suitable— miniature dachsunds, poodles, pekes, even corgis. I had no right to take Bonzo back to London. She would be couched by Davey's bed now, instead of grumbling between kitchen and living-room, if he had not shut his door. Yet I did not want to do the decent thing; I wanted to keep her.

In the morning I said, 'I think Bonzo should stay here with you.'

'Gone off her?'

I almost threw a cup of coffee at him. Why couldn't he have the grace to know what I was feeling, and to reply that Bonzo had attached herself to me, and would wish to remain with me, no matter where? I said, 'She belongs here. Alone in the flat, three days a week, London's no life for a dog.'

'She likes you.'

Too late and not strong enough. 'That's got nothing to do with it.'

'Sell her, then.'

I put the cup down carefully; it seemed safer to do so. 'You don't make it easy, do you?'

'I don't play other people's games.'

'Are you trying to tell me you don't want her? If you are, you're lying. Anyway you have to think of her welfare.'

'I'm trying to tell you she may not be safe here. I'm not staying, I tell you that. A bit of demolition down the garden, and then I'm off.'

I stared at him. 'But it's worked. You said yourself, once the secret's out, we're safe.'

'Many a slip. If it's worked, I'll come back.' The last of the folded sheets was on the kitchen table, where I had left it the night before. Davey threw it in the fire, and we watched it burn, the four men and the boy curling and blackening in the flames.

I left the cottage, with Bonzo, after breakfast in the hired car. I stopped at a newsagent's in Banbury in the Oxford Road to buy a copy of the *Radical*, but they had none. I parked the car, left Bonzo in it, and went to W. H. Smith's in the Shopping Precinct, where there would certainly be copies, but they had none. I stopped again in Oxford, leaving the by-pass and driving into the city, but could find no copies. I was told that they had not yet arrived.

There were no copies at South Kensington Underground Station, none in any of the newsagent's shops in Harrington Road and the Old Brompton Road. I went as far as Gloucester Road Station, and as I emerged from it, saw the man in the brown suit on the other side of the street, watching me. He smiled, and gave one of those half-waves that one gives to friendly acquaintances, and I crossed the road to speak to him.

'Nice try!' he said.

'What happened?'

'Sad really! The complete issue was seized when it arrived in London by officers of the Obscene Publications Squad. Taken away, all twelve thousand copies, bundled up, just as they were, and burned.'

'You didn't have to burn the copies. You could have taken out the inserts, and burned them.'

'Safer not. Untie the bundles, let stuff like that slip out, you don't know where it's going. These young police constables, easily corrupted. Sexually explicit scenes, Mr Hatcher. Deviant. Wiser not.'

'I thought you were wounded.'

He pointed to his side. 'You wouldn't believe the sticking-plaster. I should be in bed. We'll take a taxi to your flat, if you don't mind. The Department will pay.'

He had been hurt on my account, but I could not like him. We climbed the stairs very slowly, and he rested at the second landing. 'Got the negatives?'

'Yes.' I had put them back in Bonzo's collar.

'Might as well let me have them.'

'Alright.' Would he realise that photographic blocks had been made? I supposed he would. In any case, there was no way I could warn Davey, who would, I hoped, by this time have already moved on. 'They're in the flat.'

Bonzo remembered him, and backed away, wary. This time he did not insist on shaking her paw. He nodded as I removed the negatives from her collar. 'Ingenious!' He took them, counted them, held them up to the light, and stowed them away in a wallet of red leather. 'Like to tell me where you've been?'

'No.'

'I expect the Colonel will want to talk to you. There's no hurry. Give it a few days. We'll send a car.'

The *Radical* did not appeal against the seizure. The *Radical*, in fact, did rather well out of the whole business, with funding guaranteed by an anonymous source for at least another year of publication.

'You were never in any danger from us, bar a little bit of discomfort at Gatwick Airport. Had to be sure you weren't carrying the negatives with you.'

'You knew I had them?'

'No. Much more likely you didn't. No reason for you to have them. We thought the silly little bugger had tucked them away somewhere. Bloody time-bomb waiting to go off. It wasn't important, d'you see, whether you had them or not. Keeping an eye on you, that was important. The bleating of the goat excites the tiger?'

'Sorry?'

'*Stalky & Co*. Wonderful book. I re-read it every year, that and *Alice*. My wife says they did it on television, you know, sort of kids' serial, something like that. Terrible error. You wouldn't get the flavour.'

I had been made to read The Official Secrets Act, and to sign a paper stating that I had read it, and understood it, and understood the penalties which would be imposed on me if I were to go about revealing the Official Secrets which had been entrusted to me. None had, of course, been entrusted. Instead, I had stumbled across a secret, and those others who had also done so, partly because of me, had suffered an extreme penalty. It appeared, however, that I was now to be entrusted with a few ancillary secrets, of no importance, just for the form of the thing.

A car had been sent for me. I had been driven to Sydenham in an Austin Princess with tinted windows, and now confronted a man in military uniform, with medal ribbons on the breast of his jacket, who sat at a leather-topped desk with three telephones on it, and played with a gold fountain pen.

'Our chaps had two objects, d'you see. One was to find the negatives, and suppress them. Can't have that kind of thing. Does a lot of damage. Secondly, just as important, more important really, find out who'd set the whole damned business up, and suppress him.'

'The fourth man?'

'What fourth man? What does he mean, Bailey?'

Again the man in the brown suit was taking a back seat, but this time it appeared as if the seat were truly subordinate. 'The fourth man in the photos, sir, I think.'

'Oh, that fellow! Lord, no! We know all about that fellow. German fellow. Bavarian. Some sort of politicial fellow; I can't tell them apart, that lot. Quite a jolly fellow really, if you disregard his little habit. The Germans don't seem to get so het up about that sort of thing. Smack his bottom, tell him not to be a naughty boy, leave the rest to us, and quite content to do so. Wish I could say the same for our American cousins. Never seen so much botheration and running about. Sorry!'

'Smack his bottom?'

'Best way to deal with him. Won't do it again.'

I shut my eyes, and for a moment a picture formed of this preposterous figure in front of me, with his *Stalky* and his *Alice*, and just behind him the man in the brown suit, surreptitiously manipulating the strings which opened and closed the mouth of his ostensible superior. It was an act, had to be. I would have found a German politician, even a Bavarian, easily enough, either in *Stern* or the *Pictorial Who's Who*. Did they even care whether I believed them or not?

I said, 'And do you know now who the man is, the one behind it all?' What I really wanted to ask was whether they had found the blocks, and what had happened to Davey.

'We shall do. Simple now. All we have to do is work back, d'you see, from Ars Gratia Artis. Most of the smaller birds will sing, provided we can get to them before he puts them down.' Would Jerry sing, or be put down? Would Pru be put down? They must have the blocks, must have found Davey, or they would not be treating me in this casual friendly way, with coffee in bone-china cups and pink wafer biscuits. Would Davey be put down? Had he been put down already? It was as if Gavin had communicated a killing disease, of which I was the carrier. 'Point is, do you see, they didn't know any more than we did whether you had the negatives or not, but they had to get to you and find out. Piece of cake for us. Just leave you out in the open, and watch from a tree. Unsettle you a bit from time to time, to keep you bleating. Bailey looked after all that.'

I said, 'Why get himself wounded? He didn't have to rescue me. You'd found your tiger. A trail to him, anyway.'

'Conscientious chap. Won't waste good meat.'

The man in the brown suit said, 'I'd got quite fond of Mr Hatcher, sir.'

'Does you credit.'

Had they only brought me in to crow over me? Unlikely. For interrogation? But they had given information—if it *was* information—not asked for any. I said, 'You want to question me, I suppose—what's it called?—debriefing.'

'No. Owed you an explanation.'

Unlikely. They were not the kind of people to pay what they owed, unless it suited them. Keeping me quiet? The penalties of the Official Secrets Act were supposed to do that. Perhaps it was no more than a tidying instinct in them. They were, as far as I was concerned, closing the file, and wished me to know it.

I said, 'How do I know that you're telling me the truth?'

'Good queston. You don't, of course. Does it make any difference?'

Outside the door the man in the brown suit said, 'You should have stayed in Vaduz to collect that five thousand francs. It's going to take years to pay off your Access account.'

It was Thursday, November 11th, when I first looked through the kitchen window of my flat, and saw two women and a dog in a first-floor room of the house opposite, and on Thursday, April 7th, I had my interview with the superior of the man in the brown suit, a period of five months which completed my involvement with what Hitchcock called 'the McGuffin'. During those five months, I rarely felt myself to be in command of the situation, and even when I did feel myself to be so, was in reality not so. People died, were murdered in fact, probably more people than I know about, and some were innocent people (my wife, Gavin's grandmother, the photographer), and some were murdered at least partly on my account, while I myself sustained no more physical injury than a cut lip and a few bruises.

And I need never have been involved; it was only my own curiosity, my obsession with film, which carried me into the world of the McGuffin. I did no good. I changed nothing, except inasmuch as I was myself an object, a mere instrument to be used by the man in the brown suit, who would have found another object just as suitable to his purpose if he had not found me.

What is 'the McGuffin'? It is the term Hitchcock used for the object in any film which gave his principal characters their motive for action—the secret plans of the new aircraft in *The Thirty Nine Steps*, the lady herself, I suppose, in *The Lady Vanishes*. It is said that Hitchcock believed that the director need not spend much effort on it, since it was only an excuse for action, but one can see that to the characters of the story, caught up in that action, it might have much more importance, since some of them would die because of it, not as many, to be sure, as are killed over a five-month period in Northern Ireland, far fewer than in Lebanon, Chile or El Salvador, but more than are usual in South Kensington or Vaduz. My McGuffin had been the roll of negatives, which had come into my life and gone out again, leaving my circumstances (you may think) not greatly changed.

I still have the same job, with Press Shows three days a week, and, as I have noted, the *Radical* is at least temporarily on firmer financial footing. The project of combining my own students at East Hounslow with those of the Photography Course to make a detailed storyboard was highly successful, giving pleasure and a sense of achievement to both, as well as some publicity for the College, in consequence of which I have been asked to take courses at Richmond also, with the assurance of a full class, adding £25 a week for 39 weeks of the year to my income, and causing me very little extra work, since the same preparation does for both courses. My wife, rather to my surprise, had made a will, of which I was the sole beneficiary. There was not a great deal of money, but she held the flat at Holland Park on a long lease. I could have moved in, but have chosen to sell it so as to be able to buy a long lease on my own flat, to which I am accustomed.

On the debit side, the easy tears, which I had thought to have been exorcised by Davey, have come back, usually for no reason that I can discover, usually in the early evenings when I am alone, as I usualy am at that time, except for Bonzo. Also I wake early in the mornings, and cannot get back to sleep, my thoughts running over and over the same ground like squirrels in a cage. (I do not know why squirrels should be the common instances of such behaviour, when it is hardly more than a hundred years, during the time of those Victorian values so much admired by our present Prime Minister, since humans were shackled to a treadmill.) Most activity, particularly most mental activity, tires me, requiring the positive application of will-power to perform it. Do not mistake me. I do my work, all my work, meet my deadlines, but it takes more effort and gives less satisfaction, to me certainly and perhaps to my readers. My biography of Clint Eastwood has been finished, but it is not the best of my achievements in that line, and, cushioned by my wife's bequest, I have refused to tackle Richard Gere.

One must not give in to such a condition; I do not propose to live out my life on valium and anti-depressants. I have set myself the task of writing down the events of these five months, partly in the hope of doing what every creative writer does, which is use my own experience, emotions, pain if you like, as the raw material for literature, taking it from inside, putting it outside, transforming, reshaping, so that its effect will be on others, leaving myself no longer affected, and partly as a discipline, so that, having been able to write this narrative account at the rate of so many words a day for so many days, is a proof to myself that I do still function as an intelligent being.

I do function.

If our child had lived, Anne and I would still have been divorced, I think, because I should still have got on her nerves after a time. All that was not to do with our having allowed the child to die, but with Anne's having reached the end of exploring my capabilities as a human being. Both of us were to blame, if blame were in the case, she for not being able to accept what there was, I for not being able to offer something more, or at least different.

Of course I could not have looked after a child with spina

bifida, not on my own, or perhaps any child. The quality of my life, do you see, is inferior. Instead I have Bonzo.

All that is needed for survival is that one should love a single other living being, and receive love in return.

FINIS

Added to the typescript in Hatcher's own handwriting.

I think I may have recognised the fourth man in the photographs.
It was the most extraordinary thing.

AFTERWORD

OF THE FOUR MEN PHOTOGRAPHED IN THE SAUNA, THE member of Her Majesty's Government resigned from the Cabinet, was created a Life Peer, and several months later was found dead in his car, with the garage door locked from the inside, and the car engine running. Evidence was given that he had been unable to adjust to political life in the House of Lords, had become depressed, and had taken to drinking a mixture of brandy and opium, a considerable amount of which was found in his stomach at the post mortem. The N.A.T.O. general was killed, during an exercise, by a runaway tank. The president's special aide was assassinated by a heroin addict, already a victim of A.I.D.S. who had selected an aide as his victim because he was an ignorant and confused man, and had thought the one responsible for the other, or so it was said by members of the small junkie community among whom he had been living. The man was unable to speak for himself, since he was shot by a bodyguard immediately after the murder. Nothing is known of the identity or whereabouts of the fourth man.

Paul Hatcher died of food-poisoning very soon after completing his narrative. His body lay undiscovered for several days, until the tenants of the flat below complained to the landlords about the persistent howling of his alsatian dog. An empty foil container for Seafood Crumble, its 'eat-by' date long expired, was found on his kitchen table. Hatcher's obituary in *The Times* was placed fourth in a column of four.

Bonzo, the dog, was taken to Battersea Dogs' Home, where she very quickly found a new owner, a youngish man, prematurely grey.

The fat man in the trilby hat, who appeared briefly at the top of steps on page 17, died peacefully in his sleep in a hospital in Hollywood on the night of April 28th, 1980.

ABOUT THE AUTHOR

John Bowen was born in India and sent back to England at the age of six to be reared by grandparents, boarding schools, and various aunts. He returned to India during World War II and served in the army as a captain. An Oxford graduate, he writes for television and the theater when not writing novels. His plays, of which the best known is AFTER THE RAIN, have been produced on Broadway and throughout Europe.

27 million Americans can't read a bedtime story to a child.

It's because 27 million adults in this country simply can't read.

Functional illiteracy has reached one out of five Americans. It robs them of even the simplest of human pleasures, like reading a fairy tale to a child.

You can change all this by joining the fight against illiteracy.

Call the Coalition for Literacy at toll-free **1-800-228-8813** and volunteer.

**Volunteer
Against Illiteracy.
The only degree you need
is a degree of caring.**

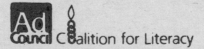

Ad Council   Coalition for Literacy

LV-3